Inside the Cave . . .

Christie held the doll upright.

"Lady Maude," Libby said. "That's the right name for her, isn't it? She looks proud and important—like she's somebody."

Lady Maude had puffs and curls of dark red hair, brown eyes, and lashes and brows of what Christie thought might be real hair, too—not just painted on. On the elaborate rolls and curls of hair perched a small hat with curled black plumes. The earrings that had been fitted into very tiny holes in her ears looked gold and showed sparks of red stones. . . . And she did have gloves on, while a swinging metal purse, very small, was clipped to the belt of her dress. Around her shoulders was a black velvet cape lined in fur, and a small muff of the same fur had been fitted over one of her hands.

Christie passed the doll to Libby and lifted up another layer of packing. The sweet sandalwood smell was strong. What lay beneath were Lady Maude's belongings. . . .

ANDRE NORTON

TEN MILE TREASURE

AN ARCHWAY PAPERBACK
Published by POCKET BOOKS • NEW YORK

AN ARCHWAY PAPERBACK *Original*

An Archway Paperback published by
POCKET BOOKS, a Simon & Schuster division of
GULF & WESTERN CORPORATION
1230 Avenue of the Americas, New York, N.Y. 10020

ISBN: 0-671-56102-2

First Archway Paperback printing July, 1981

10 9 8 7 6 5 4 3 2 1

AN ARCHWAY PAPERBACK and colophon are
trademarks of Simon & Schuster.

Printed in the U.S.A.

IL 4+

Contents

1
Ten Mile Station

It was hot, and dusty, and bumpy—very bumpy. The station wagon seemed to jump from one rut to the next. At first the desert had been exciting. Not now, Christie thought, it was rather scary the farther they drove into it. Her head ached a little as the twins kept up that everlasting game.

"Two of those cactus things—" Parky yelled almost in his sister's ear.

"Saguaro," Christie corrected. She was the one to hold the book this time around and look up all the strange things they could not name.

"Cactus things," Parky repeated stubbornly. "And a roadrunner, a cow, two cowboys, a jeep—that's all for me!" His head went from side to side, though all their luggage and the camping things were so stacked that it was hard to see out. "And"—his voice became squeaky with triumph—"a real live Indian! That ought to count up to a hundred points for me. Nobody else saw the Indian until I did!"

"I saw the great big rabbit," his twin, Perks, said quickly.

"Jackrabbit," Christie corrected again. Really, they ought to learn the proper names of things if they were going to live in this country—

"Fifty for the Indian." Neal cut Parky's claim in half. He marked the score in his notebook.

"It—he—was worth more'n fifty! That isn't fair!"

"Children!" Mother looked as far as she could over her shoulder. "If you can't play without quarreling, then just stop that game—now."

The station wagon gave an extra-hard bump. She gasped. Parky and Perks slid together with a thump, while the desert book seemed to jump right out of Christie's hold, thudding into Neal's ribs.

"What—what did we hit then?" Mother's voice sounded queer. But the car was running more smoothly again.

"Dip," Father answered. "They leave depressions in the road to drain off flash floods—but that one was deeper than most. We've only a mile more if the last direction was

2

right. This is just the old back trail—the new road will be much closer."

"I certainly hope so." Mother looked around again. "You all right, children?"

"Sure," Neal answered for them all. Christie straightened her glasses on her sweating nose.

At first this had been a big adventure, going out into the desert. Now she was not at all sure anymore. Just think of that last town—it had been marked on Father's map as the town of Ocotillo. But when they had found it, what had been there? Just a gas station, or rather an adobe building with a gas pump out in front, and inside a hamburger place and half of it a garage. It had smelled. Christie's nose wrinkled thinking of the smell—grease and oil—nasty.

What if Ten Mile Station was like that? How could they live in such a place? They couldn't—that's all. She longed to ask Neal what he thought, but she would not now with all the rest of the family listening.

Mother was depending on her to see that Parky and Perks did not get cross and start squabbling. Maybe they had played the See It game long enough after all—

What she was thinking was interrupted by a loud wail from the box wedged between her and the wall of the car. That was answered by a whine from Baron, stretched out on a blanket roll behind the twins.

Christie leaned over and tried to peek inside

3

the cat carrier through the netted window in one end. The carrier itself kept wobbling against her. Shan wanted out. He had his harness on and maybe, if she held the leash tight so he could not take one of his flying leaps, she could let him. It must be awfully hot in there. She pushed the book onto Neal's knee.

"Can't we let Shan out? I know we've the air conditioning, but he must be so hot."

At Neal's nod they did so. She needed his help—sometimes it seemed as if Shan had springs inside him, he could move so fast. Then, anchored with his leash, he sat on her knees. But his ears were flattened and he showed his teeth in a warning that he was about ready to actively protest all that was going on.

Thai Shan was a very special person, as he had long ago given the Kimballs to understand. Did they think he was going to ride in a carrier for miles and miles and days and days? In spite of Christie's coaxing words and soothing scratching behind his ears, he continued to complain at the top of his voice. That was not as shrill as that of his Siamese mother, but loud enough. He had his dark brown coat from his Burmese father and made a very handsome appearance, as he well knew.

"All right, Shan," Christie assured him. "We'll be there soon and you can discover what kind of new bugs live around here—in the grass."

4

Grass—what kind of grass would grow in a desert? When she looked out now she saw rocky walls closing in about them.

"A canyon," Neal said, though she had not asked any question.

Here there were some growing things, plants and flowers! Christie was startled by cactus plants that were wearing round crowns of color. There were bushes too, and small trees. Father was driving even more slowly, so they could see a lot more. Birds flew up as the car passed and the twins knelt on the seat to look out more easily.

"There's water here somewhere, all right," Father said.

There was something in his tone of voice that surprised Christie. Had Father been afraid there would be no *water?* For a long time few people had come out along this bumpy old road—that she did know. Now there was going to be a big new highway coming through and Ten Mile Station would be close to that.

That was the reason why they were here. It was called Ten Mile because a long time ago it had been the only water in ten miles and all the stage coaches had stopped there. Now the Kimballs were going to open it up again—not for stage coaches, but for cars, making it a place where people could stop and get food and gas and perhaps stay all night. When Father had lost his job because his company had been bought by another one, he had heard about Ten Mile and the chance to make it come alive again.

The canyon widened out and there were real trees. But the road became more and more bumpy. At last Father took one hand from the steering wheel and pointed ahead.

"There it is." The twins scrambled over Christie and Neal to see. Shan yelled and Baron barked loudly.

They were answered by a strange sound as Father stopped the car before the biggest of a group of buildings. There was a pole-walled corral to one side and in that Christie caught a glimpse of something small and brown-gray. That strange sound was coming from there. Beyond, two burros flapped their long ears, and there was a horse standing watching them.

Somehow they all piled out, almost on top of one another, to look at the station. It was a long, low building. At the bottom it was built of stone, then came thick walls of adobe, with wooden pillars in front to support an outward stretch of the roof like a porch. The windows had heavy shutters of solid slabs of wood, but those were fastened back. To Christie it did not look like a house-house at all.

Beyond the corral with the burros and the horse stood another building, and a man came out of the door of that. He was small—a lot shorter than Father—and he wore a red shirt with gray jeans and high-heeled boots. Perched toward the back of his head was a wide-brimmed hat that was as brown as the dirt of the corral. Strangest of all, he had an apron of leather tied around his waist, while he carried a big hammer in one hand.

His face was tanned nearly as brown as his dusty hat. Perhaps it looked even browner because there was a bushy white mustache across it to half hide his mouth. His thick eyebrows and some pieces of hair plastered down on his forehead were the same color.

"Howdy," he said. Then the burros brayed together and he swung swiftly round and slammed the hammer down on the top rail of the corral so that some splinters flew into the air. "Drat you, Sheba, Solomon. You keep your dang-blastered opinions to yourselves now, hear me? You folks lost?" Hardly taking a breath between words, he was speaking to Father now.

"If this is Ten Mile Station and you're Layton Odell, we're not," Father answered. "I guess you might say we're the new owners. I'm Harvey Kimball and this is my family."

"New owners? Glory be! Th'Bright Company gonna start runnin' stages again? Now if that ain't the beatenest news in a full month of Sundays! I always said as how someday they'd find out this country weren't made for those

cars what are always breakin' down or runnin' outta gas or somethin'."

Christie thought he looked at the station wagon as if he did not like it at all.

"Not the stage company," Father answered. "But the station itself—we hope to put that to work again. The new highway's going through near here, you know—"

"Sure it is," Mr. Odell interrupted. "Bustin' right through the country proper, that they are. You can hear their big diggers or such clink-clankin' all day long if the wind's in the right direction. Don't need 'em here, never did, never will. What you mean—the station's going to work again? How can it be if the company ain't goin' to run stages?"

"It will be a stop for tourists—we hope. As soon as the highway's open, there will be a lot of travel through to the park and people going to stay at the new inn on the reservation, the one the Navajo Council has agreed to. We have a license to run this as a motel."

"Station without a stage line—that don't seem right somehow." Mr. Odell shook his head. "Place is in pretty good shape though. Never was let just go back to the wild like Darringer—"

"Darringer?" Mother asked as Mr. Odell paused to squirt a stream of tobacco juice, making a black spot in the dust.

"Ghost town, ma'am—leastwise that's what

9

they call it now." Mr. Odell waved a hand in the general direction of up canyon. "Minin' town, it was. Pretty much just a heap of boards and some 'dobe walls now, I guess. Older than my time and I've been around a sight longer than most people would guess. Now I can remember when I was a size to them two"—he jerked a thumb at the twins—"how the stage was still runnin' through here. M'pa, he was the stationmaster—the last one. Kept on here when they closed 'cause he had a diggin' that was still showin' color enough to grubstake us regular. Then the company, they gave him a bit to keep things up—had somethin' to do with their holdin' claim to the land as long as some agent of theirs stayed on.

"I did some ridin' for the Bar Six, learned me the smithin' trade, did a bit of prospectin', and then thought as how I'd take up the old station. Ain't heard nothin' from the company for years now. But I've kept things goin'—nobody bothers me and I don't go huntin' around for anybody to bother." He stopped short and looked at Father as if he suddenly thought of something unpleasant. "But if you're the top man now, then—"

"Then you stay right on—if it suits you, Mr. Odell. It would be a help we need, since you know more about the place than we certainly do," Father said quickly.

"Well, now, that I probably do. No need to

10

stand here gabbin' neither—like nothin' needs gettin' done. I don't bunk down in the main house—my quarters are back yonder." He waved the hammer toward the smaller building from which he had come. "Only I do give it a sweep out now and then. Maybe it ain't clean enough to suit a lady, ma'am. But you just say what you want done, and if it can be did, it will be. Sure good to see the old Ten Mile come to life again—so it is!"

The next hours were busy. Layton Odell showed them proudly around. Inside the big building was first a long room with a fireplace at one end and at the other a sink, with a pump attached, beside an old-fashioned iron stove. Three doors along the wall, facing the front door, opened into two smaller rooms that had bunks built in and one much larger one with six bunks.

"Drivers' quarters—" Mr. Odell said of one of the smaller rooms. "The others for passengers. This—" he opened the door of the second small room wider—"was for ladies. Didn't get many womenfolk traveling most times, I guess. Gents—they bedded down in the big room. Ten Mile was an overnight stop most times."

There were washstands, too, in the rooms— each with a big china bowl and pitcher standing on top.

Parky pulled at Christie's arm. "Where's the bathroom, Chris?"

"I don't think there is one," she whispered back uncertainly. She had put Shan down and he was tugging at his leash, sniffing at corners as if something of interest must have been there recently. Mice? Christie, just looking around, could well believe in mice.

"But you *do* have to have bathrooms in the house!" protested Parky. "It must be some-where—"

"You don't have them in camps." Neal had come up behind them. "This is like a camp—in a way—" But his sentence trailed off as if he were beginning to have some doubts of his own.

"Now you've got water here—mighty fine water." Mr. Odell led the way to the sink and was working the pump handle up and down vigorously. A stream of water gushed out sud-denly, spraying even beyond the edges of the sink basin to spatter onto the floor. "Holds even in dry spells. Good and cold—worth more'n a good strike in the long run—water is in this country."

Mother looked at the pump with an odd expression on her face. She put her hand out into the stream and jerked it quickly back again, her expression now one of surprise.

"It *is* cold, Harvey! Almost as if it had been iced!"

"Whole place is cool, too—" Father stood with his hands on his hips, looking eagerly about the big room. "These thick walls must provide real insulation against the heat."

"Them walls *are* thick," Mr. Odell agreed. "Made to keep the heat out in summer, cold in winter. This place was built good, all right. Best station, they always said, on the whole danged run. Pa told me that plenty times, and he was right. Now, I got me a mare with a shoe ready to be set on. I'll go and finish that job off and then I'll be back to help with any fetchin', ma'am, as you may want."

"That's kind of you—to want to help, Mr. Odell—" Mother began, when he paused at the outer door and shook his head at her.

"Ma'am, Mr. Odell—that don't sound right, it really don't. Most folks call me Pinto." He took off his hat for the first time and his white hair fluffed up like a bushy wig. "Don't show it anymore, but when I was a youngun, I had two-color hair—black with a big white patch clean center, 'bout here—" He poked a finger up from his forehead a little to the right. "Born with it, I was. So they took to callin' me Pinto and it stuck. Sounds more like me than Mr. Odell."

"Very well." Mother smiled. "I'll remember, Pinto. But it is kind of you to offer to help."

"Mom, can we go to see the horse getting a shoe put on? Please, Mom. We never saw a horse getting shoes before." Parky and Perks closed in from either side to tug at Mother's slacks.

"Perhaps Mr.—Pinto doesn't want you to bother him."

"Let 'em come, if they want to, ma'am. Can't be any more bother than them danged burros, and I've had them a-breathin' down my neck many a time. Say, girl, that's a mighty strange-lookin' cat you got there. I don't remember ever seein' his like before."

Shan had come into a patch of sunlight that showed through the dusty window, and his rich brown color was like that of a chocolate bar, dark and thick. He turned his head to regard Pinto with eyes that were neither green or blue but a color Mother always called aquamarine.

"I'm Christie." She did not quite like being called "girl." "And he's Thai Shan—that means Prince Shan. He's half Siamese—half Burmese."

Pinto had clapped his hat on again. "Don't never remember hearin' of such before. But he's sure a handsome critter, ain't he? Knows it, too, I reckon, if I'm any judge. Well, come along, all you who want to see Susie get a new shoe—"

"Mother?" Christie hesitated.

Mother was nodding. "Go ahead, Christie, and you, too, Neal—just keep an eye on the twins. We have to do some planning anyway before we begin to unload the car."

They all had their assigned unloading duties, but if Mother said those could be put off, Christie was as eager as the twins to go exploring. Picking up Shan, in spite of his protests, she hurried out to try and catch up with Perks and Parky, who had burst out-of-doors with yells of pleasure. Neal followed more slowly. He had his notebook in one hand and his pen in the other. Christie, catching a glimpse of those, slowed. She had an idea of what might be in his mind now, and it reminded her of what had become—at least between the two of them— the Big Plan.

Of course, they had heard enough before they started west to make them understand how much the success of the Ten Mile Station would mean to all the Kimballs. Mother and Father had talked about it a lot. Sometimes maybe they even forgot Neal and Christie might be doing homework at the desk in the living room and so be able to overhear. Because there could be trouble. Things never went smoothly— Christie knew that herself. You could plan for something and have it all spoiled by a happening you had not counted on at all. She understood as well as Neal that Mother and Father were worried at times.

But the Big Plan—that was something else, something that Neal had mentioned first and Christie had seen right away was important, even if it were something Mother and Father had never spoken about at all.

The idea had come first five days ago, when they had begun the long drive from Ohio to Arizona. On the first night out Perks and Parky had been wild to stop at a motel where they had had a lot of pheasants and other birds in a wire enclosure and kept advertising that show along the road for miles before the station wagon finally got there. From then on the twins, then Neal and Christie, had kept watching for motel signs. Not just the kind that read TV IN EVERY ROOM or SWIMMING POOL, but others with wayside zoos (though Mother did not like those and said it was cruel to keep wild animals shut up so). But one in Missouri had shown a lot of things from the Civil War days, and there had been another where a real live buffalo had a pasture all to himself and they could watch him.

So it became the Plan. They—Christie and Neal, and the twins—were to find something to show that would make Ten Mile Station a place where people would just *have* to stop and see what was there. That would probably keep them long enough to eat, or to get gas, or even stay overnight. But whatever they showed had to be important—and different—exciting enough to make the tourists stop first. So the children had been making lists of ideas, which Neal carefully kept in the back of his notebook. So far,

Christie was afraid, none of them were very bright ideas worthy of a real Big Plan.

Baron was by the corral waiting for them. Now he stood up, his creamy tail wigwagging his excitement and delight at being in this place of unusual and exciting smells, wide open to give pleasure to a dog. He was a very large Shepherd with silver cream fur, except that his back was marked with a black saddle. Now he trotted forward, his tongue lolling happily from his jaws, to escort Neal and Christie to where they could look between the poles of the corral at its inhabitants.

There was a baby burro with the two big ones! Christie held Shan firmly as the small creature threw back his head and loosed a sound much bigger than himself. The horse was a very ordinary-looking brown one with a black mane and tail. And they had seen other burros, but never a baby one.

"Is he good enough to fit into the Plan?" Christie asked her brother.

After a long moment, he nodded slowly. "Maybe for a start."

They went on with Baron to the shed where Pinto was fitting a shoe to the hoof of another horse. The twins were squatting down on their heels watching, round-eyed.

"Doesn't it hurt her?" Perks wanted to know, her face screwed up in sympathy. "Not even when you nail it right on like that?"

17

"No sirree. It would hurt old Susie more to go walkin' over these rocky trails without no shoes. She was limpin' bad yesterday 'cause she had throwed the old shoe. This don't hurt her none—just makes her feet safe. There now, ol'gal, you're a sight better off now, ain't you, than when you was goin' around three-legged this mornin'?" He slapped the mare on the flank, untied her rope hackamore, and led her out into the corral.

"Please." Christie was at his elbow as he put the gate bars back in place. "What's its name —the baby burro, I mean?"

"That's Jericho. He's named that rightly 'cause he's got a bray what'd bring down Jericho walls were he to come close to 'em—them soldiers what took the place in th'old days, they'd never have had to use their trumpets were he marchin' alongside 'em. You know the Bible story about those trumpets and how the walls came all tumblin' down? My ma used to read that to me when I was a little'un. I always favored the excitin' stories an' she knew it."

"Yes, we know," Parky answered before Christie could. "He's Jericho—and this is Baron." He thumped one dusty hand down on the dog's dark back. "He's a real, true police dog—been to school and has papers that says so! And that's my sister Perks." He waved toward his twin with much less ceremony.

18

"Your sister now!" Pinto stared from one twin to the other in open-faced surprise.

Christie sighed. When would the twins ever decide that Parky was a boy and Perks a girl? So far their insistence on identical shirts, jeans, and floppy haircuts had caused a lot of confusion in school and out.

"Their real names," she explained, "are Patrick and Patricia—"

"Parky and Perks," cut in Parky with a scowl and an elbow cocked outward, which Christie managed to avoid with a quick half-turn developed in long practice. "He's Neal and we're all Kimballs, like Dad said. Now"—he grinned, showing a new toothless gap in front—"we're introduced and can be friends. What's that horse's name?"

He pointed to the brown one who appeared to be asleep standing right there.

"Old Timer. And an old-timer he is—'most as old, judgin' by horse time, as I am. He's got a right to take things easy these days."

"Do you ride him?" Parky wanted to know.

"Not much anymore. He's a mite old for any trailin'. Was a top ropin' horse in his day. I bought him offen the Bar Six when they thought him past his work. He'n me, we worked together real good once, and I like to think he has it easy now. Susie carries me where I want to go these days."

Pinto turned and was looking at the dust-covered station wagon. "Your folks have a proper lot of stuff to unpack. Suppose we go and see if they need help doin' it now."

"Mr.—Pinto," Christie corrected herself hastily, "do you live here all alone—with just the animals? Isn't there anyone else around?"

"Not generally. Oh, there's some as come and neighbors now and then. The Wildhorses— it's 'bout time for them to be showin' up."

"Wild horses! You mean real wild horses— like on TV?" For the first time Neal lost his usual calm. "Gee, can you rope them—catch them and tame them?"

Pinto threw back his head and gave a bark of laughter that sounded near as loud as Jericho's bray. "Not these kinda Wildhorses. 'Course they was wild once—or their old folks were—accordin' to our ideas. These Wildhorses—they're people—Navajos. Wildhorse is their last name—like yours is Kimball and mine's Odell. Mighty good neighbors, they are. Not like some what were around here in the past. Just you looky here now—"

He led the way to one of the thick wooden shutters and loosed the catch that held it back against the wall of the house, swinging it out so they could see what he was now pointing to clearly. Sticking out of the wood was a piece of stone and just above it a second gray splinter.

"Know what those be?" Pinto tapped his forefinger against the lower stone. That's a genuine injun war arrowhead! Fired right into this here bit of plank by some Apache come raidin'. This station—twice it was a fort, held against raidin' parties. I heard m'pa tell 'bout them. In those times injuns weren't no good neighbors to us, and sure as shootin' we didn't favor them none either. Plenty faults on both sides, as I heard it. M'pa, he fought Injuns, but he fed 'em too, when they was starvin' 'cause they was chased up this way and penned in on land where even coyote couldn't get hisself a good meal. But them were the old days—things are different now. Only they did have two-three fights hereabouts, and you can find yourself arrow points to prove it.''

Christie clutched at Neal's arm eagerly and saw him staring back at her with beginning excitement. This was the best idea yet for the Big Plan.

2
New Neighbors

Birds awoke Christie the next morning with their cries. She lay in the bunk listening until she suddenly wanted to get up and be out and crawled from beneath the covers. Shan leaped from where he had been curled between the edge of her pillow and the rough wall and padded to the door. He looked back at her with a demanding sound deep in his throat. Christie dressed with more speed than she usually did in the mornings and tiptoed past Perks, still asleep in the opposite bunk.

In the big outer room there were a lot of shadows, and the doors to both the other rooms were closed. Baron was scratching and whining from behind the one that was shut on the boys' room and she let him out. The big dog touched noses with the cat and they both stood impatiently now by the outer door, watching her.

Christie snapped on Shan's leash before she unbarred the entrance way. Though the sky was light, she could not yet see the sun. A shattering sound made her jump and sent Shan, his ears flat against his head, to take refuge between her feet. For the second time that bray came from the corral. Could that really be *Jericho?*

Baron barked sharply and trotted over to look in between two of the poles. He barked again, as if warning Jericho against making such rude noises. Christie laughed and there was a flash of gray along the top pole over Baron's head. The dog ran along, leaping up now and then to try and catch the runner. Then the small animal vanished and he was left standing on his hind legs, taking great sniffs of air.

"Rroow—" Shan cried, and Christie scooped him up. He made a soft, chittering cry as a bird swooped overhead.

"Well, now, you're up bright and early."

Pinto was coming up to the corral, a rope coiled over one arm. He grinned at Christie. "Goin' to be a right good day." Throwing back his head, he squinted up at the sky from under the wide brim of his battered hat. Seeing Pinto made Christie remember what she and Neal had talked about last night.

"Mr.—Pinto—you said that there had been

a lot of Indian fights around here. Do you suppose we can find some arrowheads? Not just the ones stuck in the shutters, but loose?''

Pinto was opening the swinging gate of the corral. ''Shouldn't wonder. Except you'd have to go lookin' for them careful. And this is somethin' to keep in mind, Christie—you and them other young'uns—you don't go wanderin' off by yourselves here. 'Tain't safe. You don't know nothin' 'bout readin' trail signs, nor findin' your way 'round yet. This is no kinda country to get lost in. You stay close by where you can see the station—understand now!'' His voice was just like Father's when he said something important. Christie nodded.

''You mean— Are there bad things—bears, maybe—or wolves?'' She tried to think of any dangerous animals listed in the desert book.

''You don't have to be afraid of animals so much. Maybe there might be a big cat or two back in the canyons. Not that he'd have any mind to go stalkin' you—he'd rather have a deer or such like. No wolves in this country. And coyotes, now, they don't go botherin' nobody. But there's snakes and they ain't so friendly minded. Just gettin' lost is bad enough. So you stay where you can see the station 'cept when you got your pa or me or your ma 'round.''

Christie nodded again, even more vigorously. The warning about snakes was one that stuck in her mind. Now she watched Pinto rope the mare Susie. The three burros were drinking noisily from a hollowed-out log trough and the other horse still looked asleep standing up.

When Pinto had the mare saddled, he threw another rope around Old Timer's neck and the horse opened his eyes and reluctantly ambled forward at the slow pull. Pinto, now mounted, looked once more at Christie.

"Old Timer gets a mornin' out grazin'. You want to go along. Can't say as how Susie would take to carrying that cat of yours, though."

"Shan will stay on the leash here. He's used to that," Christie answered eagerly. "Just wait a minute."

She hurried to anchor the leash to one of the porch supports, then came flying back to be boosted up on Old Timer's back, catching fast hold of the horse's rough mane.

"First time I ever rode a horse," she admitted nervously as Pinto urged Susie ahead and Old Timer plodded behind.

"That a fact? Well, now, we'll have to see as how you learn to do that before the summer is over."

Christie was not quite sure she wanted to learn more. When she dared to look beyond

"Old Timer gets a mornin' out grazin'. You want to go along. Can't say as how Susie would take to carrying that cat of yours, though."

the mane and was glad they were going no faster.

Susie and her rider picked a path that wound around between trees, through high brush, to come out at last in a big, open space. The mare halted and, as Old Timer slow-footed up beside her, Pinto reached over and took Christie from her perch, setting her behind him. Then he twitched the rope from Old Timer's neck and the horse dropped his head and began grazing.

"Right pretty, ain't they?" Pinto pointed ahead and Christie saw trees in bloom. "Them's apricot and some peaches. Kinda old now, but still got life in 'em. The Company had an orchard and a garden here—raised their own garden sass and a lotta grub. Set a good table, the station did. My ma, she used to dry apricots, make peach leather. Mighty tasty!"

"Was the stage line still running then?" Christie held Pinto's belt with the same grip she had kept on Old Timer's mane.

" 'Bout seventy years ago now, it was—yes, they were running it. There were mines back up there"—he pointed to the rocky walls in the distance—"and the stage ran through to Darringer. Took out gold dust, brought in passengers and mail. But it started a lot earlier than even Pa's time. Back in eighteen-sixty Bright made the first run. Them were the big days. M'pa, he started ridin' shotgun a little later when he weren't more'n a kid. But he was mighty handy with his gun, and he could take over the leathers too—drive stage—if there was a need. Took a man as knowed how to drive real good to manage a six-horse team at a run. 'Tweren't till he met my ma and got married that he settled down to keep station. She didn't take to him drivin'. Though keepin' station in Apache country weren't so safe neither.

"Now—we'd better be gettin' back. Your ma wakes up to find you gone and she might be thinkin' as how you were lost."

They heard Baron barking, loud excited barks.

"Somebody must be coming." Christie knew what those barks meant.

"So? Maybe that truck from out of town with the things your pa's expectin'. Though it's a mite early for them."

Susie broke into a lope and Christie gasped, holding Pinto's belt as if her fingers were glued to the leather. She was glad they did not have to go far.

When they reached the station, she saw Baron standing in front of the door, barking furiously. Shan had retreated as far as he could—his tail was puffed up and he was spitting. Another car had pulled up beside the station wagon.

Car? No, it was a truck—or was it a trailer-camper? It looked, Christie thought, as if someone had seen a trailer and then built something like it on a truck body. And it was painted brilliant blue with patches of yellow here and there. Attached behind it was a horse trailer.

"Lucas!" Pinto stopped Susie by the corral and handed down Christie, who ran to catch Baron's collar, keeping him from rushing at the people getting out of the cab of the truck.

There was a man wearing jeans and a red shirt, the tails hanging outside. He had a hat like Pinto's, only it was newer and black and there was a band of silver discs around the crown. There was a big buckle of the same metal on the belt he wore over his shirt and he had a heavy necklace of silver set with blue stones.

He pushed back his hat a little and looked at Pinto very solemnly, raising the other hand palm out and saying, "How!"

Pinto laughed, "How, Lucas. Glad to see you, ma'am," he added to the lady who dropped from the opposite side of the cab. She wore jeans and boots, too, and a shirt of deep orangy yellow. Her long black hair was fastened back with a silver clip and she had on two jingly necklaces.

"Pinto," she called, "you just get younger every year instead of older. My"—she threw out her arms and took a deep breath—"it's good to get back!"

Two more travelers were tumbling out. One was a boy who looked to be about Neal's age.

He had on jeans, boots, and a red shirt like his father's, but he was bareheaded and his thick black hair was a rather untidy-looking mop. The girl behind him came more slowly, staring at Christie. She had a blue shirt and a necklace like her mother's, and her hair lay in two smooth braids over her shoulders.

"Something new! Pinto, don't tell me you have taken to wheels at last!" The man looked at the station wagon.

"Ten Mile's startin' up again. That's the new owner's." Pinto dropped Susie's reins to the ground and came across the yard. "Here's Christie Kimball." He nodded at Christie. "Her family's goin' to make this into a highway stop for that danged road when they get it finished."

"Christie"—now he spoke to her—"these folks are the Wildhorses I was talkin' 'bout a while back. There's Lucas and Marina, Toliver and Libby."

The Wildhorses were no longer smiling. Instead they had drawn together by their home on wheels. Lucas glanced from Christie to the station.

"Maybe we'd better pull on, Pinto. Didn't hear about the change—"

Just then the door opened and Father came out. Pinto again introduced the newcomers. Father held out his hand.

"Glad to see new neighbors. Simpson told

me that you planned to spend the summer near here."

"We did," Lucas answered. "But if the station is starting up we can make other plans—"

"Nonsense!" Father said quickly. "You have a better right to be here than the rest of us, if the truth be told. Patricia," he called, "come and meet our neighbors."

So they had breakfast together, Mother and Mrs. Wildhorse working to prepare it. Christie eyed Libby and Toliver shyly. She did not get up courage to speak until the Navajo girl knelt to admire Shan. The twins and Neal had already drawn closer to see Toliver's knife in its beaded sheath, eagerly listening to him tell about the horse that had just been transferred from their trailer to the corral.

"I never saw a cat like this before," Libby said.

"His name's Thai Shan. He's Siamese and Burmese both," Christie answered in a rush of words. "That's a lot different from most cats. Look! He really likes you."

Shan had stopped washing a paw to sniff at the hand Libby held out to him. Then he rubbed his head back and forth against her fingers.

"Scratch him behind the ears and under his throat. That's what he likes best," Christie suggested.

"I had a cat once," Libby volunteered. "But

when we traveled around so much she got lost.
I missed her a lot.''

"Do you live in the truck van all the time?"
Christed wanted to know.

"Mostly, except in the middle of the winter.
My father is a geologist, only right now he's
working for the Navajo Tribal Council, keeping
in touch with all the herders out on the range
in between his prospecting. He does a lot of
things—writes pieces for magazines, goes rock
hunting, now he's writing a history of our people. He doesn't like to live inside a town.
Mother paints pictures. They have shows of
them sometimes. She even had a show all by
herself last winter and a lot of people came and
bought them. That was exciting. They inter-
viewed her on TV, too.''

"You don't—" Christie hesitated, and then
spoke frankly. "You aren't like what I thought
Indians are." Then she flushed. What a dumb,
rude thing to say! She was sorry. But Libby
was smiling instead of looking mad.

"We're Navajos, all right, but my mother
and father went to college back east. My father
was an officer in the army, too. But this is our
real home country and we like it best here. We
are truly of the Dineh—the People—even if we
don't always stay on the reservation. Mother
and I, we have Navajo dresses. We wear them
when we visit with our people, but not when
we travel. Those wide skirts are not good for

31

climbing in and out of the van. Are you going to live here now?"

"I don't know," Christie admitted.

Libby looked sober now. "Yes—maybe Mr. Toner won't let you."

"Who is Mr. Toner?" Christie demanded in surprise. She had not heard that name before in all the talk between Father and Mother.

"He has a ranch, over there—" Libby pointed eastward with her chin as she still patted Shan. "He's been wanting to get this valley for a long time—because of the water. He's always riding over and trying to get Pinto to move out. But Pinto has some kind of a paper that says he has a right to stay here for some years. It belongs to the stage company still, so Mr. Toner has had to wait. Only he said a couple of months ago that this year Pinto's paper wasn't any good anymore and now he'd get the land. He wants it very badly."

"Well, he can't get it," returned Christie firmly. "My father has it now."

"He won't give up easily." Libby did not look so sure. "You'll see. He'll come over again—probably with Marlene."

"Who's Marlene?"

"His daughter." Libby's answer was very short and something in her tone made Christie feel that the Navajo girl did not like Marlene in the least.

Neal and Toliver, with the twins trailing them, joined the girls.

"Listen here, Chris, it's about the Plan." Neal was plainly excited. "Toliver, he thinks he knows where we can get some good arrowheads. Maybe it was one of those places where they had a fight in the old days."

The Navajo boy nodded. "Come on over to the bus," he said. "I can show you some we picked up last year. Remember, Libby, down that side wash?"

Shan had stuck his claws into Libby's shirt for anchorage and was standing on his hind feet. She put her arm around the cat. "Can we take him with us?" she asked Christie.

"If we keep him on the leash. He might stray off and get lost."

"You mean he'll walk on a leash—like a dog?" Toliver asked. "I never knew a cat would do that."

"Siamese cats will. We taught Shan to when he was just a kitten. We didn't want to lose him and back home we lived on a street where there were a lot of cars passing all the time—he could have run out and been killed."

She clipped on the leash and they all went to the truck-van. Toliver climbed inside and returned with a box in his hand. He led the way to the shadow of a tree and they all dropped down to watch him take out his discoveries.

"This is a spearhead, and these are arrowheads—you can see that by the size. Look here, see this real small one—it's really made of hard bone and was probably for hunting birds. And this is a knife, only the point is broken.''

"You want to collect arrowheads?" Libby asked Christie.

"Well—" For a moment Christie hesitated. The Plan was sort of a private thing. But apparently Neal had already told Toliver, so it did not matter if she explained to Libby.

"You see, it's really part of a plan Neal and I have. Getting the station started and making people want to stop here when the new road is open—that is important. We started watching the different motels as we came. Some had advertised swimming pools and TVs and all the usual things. But here we can't have a swimming pool and I don't know about TVs either. But other motels had special things made up to make you want to stop and see them—"

"Yes," Parky interrupted. "One had a lot of birds—big fancy ones in an outside cage. And there was another with a buffalo—honest, a real live buffalo! He was eating grass in a field and you could watch him."

"Those places," Christie went on, "put out signs for miles ahead about what you could see. We stopped at two places just because of the signs. So if we could have something special to show here, something we could put up a sign to tell about, then more people might want to stop. That's our plan—to find the right things to show."

"Last night"—Neal looked up from the broken knife he was holding—"Pinto showed us two arrowheads stuck in one of the window shutters. He said they were shot in there during an Apache raid. Well, everyone likes stories about the Old West. If we could show a lot of Indian things—"

"Old Indian things," Christie interrupted him quickly. "Not Indians today. We don't mean—" She again felt as if she might be saying the wrong thing.

Toliver laughed. "You afraid we'd think you believe we still go around raiding? That was all a long time ago. My dad always says we have to forget a lot of bad things, both you people and us. But maybe you have got a good idea, talking about the history of the Apache raids here and all. Anyway, we can take you to the place where we found these, and maybe there are more. You could think about getting other things too—like those they kept in the station in the old days. What you really ought to have is a real stagecoach to set up by the corral. That would be worth seeing!"

"Gollee!" Parky cried. "A real stagecoach! That sure would be keen. Could we, Neal, could we?"

His brother shook his head. "No such luck

as that. We had better plan on what we can find— Is this arrow place far from here? How do we get to it?"

Just then Christie remembered Pinto's warning, the one he had given her only that morning. "Pinto said we have to keep in sight of the station. He told me it was easy to get lost out there and there were snakes and—"

She saw Neal frown, but Toliver spoke first.

"It isn't far. We've been there lots of times. So you couldn't get lost if you went with us. Maybe we can do it soon—" He seemed nearly as eager as Neal looked.

"Why not go now?" demanded Parky. Perks crowded up beside him as if she was ready to take off as soon as her twin made a move. Parky did most of the talking, but Perks was all ready to back him up in any action.

"No. You know we've got to help here— unpacking," Christie reminded them, though she, too, would have liked to follow Parky's suggestion. "The truck with all our furniture is coming out from town today. And mother has to go in to shop. She has a big, long list of things—she keeps adding to it all the time. We can't go today."

Parky looked entirely unconvinced. But he knew better than to start off without Neal or Christie. He had done that once during this trip, only to lose himself and Perks. What Father had said to him when they had been found after two hours of anxious search had impressed one fact on him—he was never to go off again without one of the older children along.

"Someone is coming down the road." Toliver had turned his head to listen. Baron raced away from where he had been standing by Neal to loose a flurry of loud barks. They could see the dust rising from the rutted road now as another truck pulled along toward them through the entrance of the canyon. Christie ran to the house to announce its arrival and the whole of the station erupted into action as if it were the old days and a stage were pulling in with cargo and passengers needing instant attention.

Lucas Wildhorse drove their truck-van on past the corral to park it in a stretch of field beyond, clearing a space so the men could unload. Boxes and cartons were pulled out, carried in, or left stacked on the dirt-floored porch.

Libby and Toliver had gone off to help with their own settling in, and the four young Kimballs found that there was certainly plenty to do. At last, right after a hasty lunch, Mother took Parky and Perks, whose help was often closer to hindrance, and drove off in the station wagon for supplies. Pinto and Father went back and forth, transporting boxes, prying open crates, and Christie and Neal carried until their arms were tired, usually putting things in the wrong places so they had to be moved again.

There was a lot that had to be done to the

station house, as well as having motel cottages built as soon as workmen would come. But there Lucas Wildhorse was a help.

In the late afternoon he saddled up his horse and rode off cross country to locate Navajos who were willing to work. None of the Kimballs at this time had much to think about except getting their new home in order, and the Plan had to be pushed to the back of both Christie's and Neal's mind.

It was harder work than they had ever known, this getting things into order. Christie made sandwiches and heated coffee on the stove after Pinto had stopped long enough to light it for her. She was very tired and more than glad to see the station wagon returning near sundown with Mother. Everything still seemed to be in a dreadful muddle, she thought as she sat down thankfully, Shan draped across her knees. It certainly was going to be a long time before everything was in place. Even then, she wondered, would the station ever seem like home?

3
Up the Canyon

"If you really want to be a help, Christie, you can take the twins, and Baron—and Shan—and get them all out of here." Mother was tying on the scarf that kept the dust out of her hair and looking about the big room of the station at the same time early the next morning. There was a frown line between her eyebrows, as if she were seeing a great many things that ought to be done all at once.

"Take our lunch maybe," Christie suggested, "and have a picnic?"

"Now that's a good idea, Chris. There is enough peanut butter and jelly and those big buns left over from last night to make sandwiches. I'm sure there're bananas and—just take what you can find. But remember—don't go too far. And don't let the twins out of your sight! You might ask Neal to go with you—if Father does not need him."

Christie gathered food supplies and went to work. Buns were spread, and there were apples as well as bananas. On another shelf she found half a box of cookies. All could be packed into a basket. Nor did she forget the dry cat food in a sandwich bag, and she dumped the contents of an opened can of dog food into another such container. There—she had everything. Basket secure on her arm, and Shan scuttling ahead on his leash, she went to round up the twins.

There was plenty of noise and confusion out in the yard. Shan tried to get back into the house again, and Christie got several new claw scratches on hands and arms before she fixed him firmly under one arm. The men who had come out from town this morning to begin the job of changing some of the outbuildings into motel rooms and to lay the foundations for cottages, plus some Navajos, doing all sorts of odds and ends of unpacking and getting ready places for the building materials, the first of which were to be delivered today, were everywhere. Christie found the twins by almost falling over them where they crouched watching.

"Come on—"

"No!" Parky did not even look up at her. But Perks saw the picnic basket and pulled at her brother's arm until he shook off her hold.

"Where, Chris?" Perks asked.

"On a picnic—" Then an idea struck her—
one that might make even Parky come will-
ingly. "We'll go and ask Toliver and Libby
about hunting arrowheads— "

Parky did look up now. "You mean that?"

"If they can come. Let's go and see. Bring
Baron too." She looked for Neal, but he was
nowhere to be seen. Better not wait to hunt
him up—Parky might change his mind again.
Perks caught at Baron's collar and towed the
big dog toward the meadow where the Wildhorse van was parked.

There was Neal with Toliver. Libby was sitting on the wide driver's seat of the truck, sewing. She laid aside her lapful of material and
slid down when she saw Christie coming.

"We've got a picnic." Christie held the basket for them to see. "Mother says we ought to
keep away from the station right now while
everybody is working. Could we go and hunt
arrowheads, if the place is not too far away?"

"Taking the kids, too?" Neal demanded.

Parky stopped, his lower lip pushed out a
little as he scowled up at his brother.

"Me'n Perks, we can look for arrowheads
just the same as you! Maybe a lot better—so
there, Neal Kimball!"

"Mother said—" Christie began.

"Oh, all right. What about it, Toliver? Can
we all go there or is it too far?"

"Not far," the Navajo boy answered. "Libby,

get the canteens. We'll need to carry water—
none up there. Take some grub, too—''

When they set out on their promised expe-
dition, Toliver took the lead as guide. He wore
a small camp ax at his belt, as well as his ever-
present knife, and carried two canteens strung
on straps over his shoulders. Neal had two
more canteens and a flashlight—though why he
bothered with that in daytime, Christie did not
know—except it was his big camp one and he
was proud and careful of it.

Libby had added more food to the basket that
she and Christie now carried between them.
The twins were in the middle, where their el-
ders could keep an eye on them.

They crossed the meadow where Old Timer,
Susie, and all the visiting Navajo horses were
grazing. Then Toliver turned into a narrow way
where big rocks had fallen from the top of the
canyon wall, so that they had to twist and turn
to get around these.

Baron suddenly flashed ahead, barking loudly.
Christie hoped he was only after a rabbit—not
anything larger. What had Pinto said about ''big
cats''? The dog was hidden by the rocks now
and his barks echoed loudly. Ahead was a very
narrow space between two huge boulders and
Toliver disappeared that way, Neal right behind
him.

"Is that a cave?" Christie slowed a little.

"No," Libby told her. "It's open beyond.

My father thinks someone was blasting back in here a long time ago, maybe trying to open up a way to a mine. It's narrow, but you'll see— it comes out out all right.''

It was difficult in some places to wriggle through, and they had to tug once or twice at the basket. Shan pushed and kicked so in Christie's hold, that she had to let Libby take both handles while she controlled him. However, once they were through that rocky part there was another wide-open space before them.

This was different from the meadow—more like the desert. There were clumps of narrow, swordlike leaves gathered around tall stalks that carried weights of cream white flowers. Farther on was a barrel cactus that stood nearly as tall as Father, and nearby were two saguaroes, also in bloom. The ground underfoot was dry and crumbled when you walked on it. Just to look around made Christie suddenly feel thirsty.

Baron was standing with his front feet braced against the canyon wall, still barking loudly at a crevice several inches above his head. Toliver swung up on a rock and leaned over to peer into the same break in the stone.

"Just an old chuckawalla," he reported.

"What's a chuckawalla?" Parky wanted to know.

"Big old lizard. You chase him into a hole

like this one and he puffs himself up so he fills all the space. Then you can't pull him out. He won't hurt you—all he wants is to be left alone." Toliver slid down from his perch. "Now—" He turned his head slowly, studying the rocky walls that stretched out in a wide curve from the entrance way. "We found our points about over there. They might have been washed down in some flood, though." He gestured to the right.

Christie made Shan's leash fast to the handles of the basket Libby had already set down and let him go, sucking the last bleeding scratch he had left across the back of her hand. He crouched there on the sand staring about him in dark suspicion, wearing what the children called his "goblin look."

The boys shed their canteens, Toliver stopping to test the corking of each carefully, making a pile with the basket. Parky and Perks started to dart away and Christie had to move fast to catch up with them.

"Toliver," she called, "what about snakes?"

"Never saw any here. You kids"—he turned and faced the twins, his face as stern as Father's could be sometimes—"don't you go wandering off now. You stick with us, understand?"

For just a moment Parky looked as if he might argue as he usually did. But, perhaps because it was Toliver and not Christie or Neal who had given that order, he did not protest. He even walked instead of ran to reach the stretch of gravel and sand that might once have been the bed of a stream.

The Navajo boy squatted down on his heels, studying the gravel closely. "We found those points right about here. They get mixed up with the stones, so you have to look hard to see them."

Christie sat down, took off her glasses, and mopped her hot face. Here the sun beat down seemingly twice as hard. She wished Baron would stop barking at that chuckawalla thing. His noise hurt one's ears.

"I found one! I found one!" Perks cried, fanning one arm in the air, her hand closed tight about her treasure.

"No! You let me see it! I bet you didn't. I just bet you didn't!" Parky's jealous protest drowned her out as he sprang at his sister and tried to catch her hand.

"It's mine! I found it! Chris, don't let him take it! It's mine!" Perks threw herself back to elude her twin and jumped a drift of gravel to reach her sister. Once at Christie's side, she opened her hand to display a triangle of reddish stone. Toliver came to inspect it critically.

"It's broken—see— It could be the end of a spear point, maybe, or an extra-large arrowhead. But you're right, Perks, it is a real find!"

"Huh, just an old broken one—" Parky snorted.

However, Perks refused to be disappointed. "I found it first and it's real!" she repeated. Rubbing it back and forth across the leg of her jeans she brushed the last grain of sand from it and then stowed the piece away in her shirt pocket.

Neal made the next discovery—a perfect arrowhead this time. But Toliver turned up something else—a piece of black cord that broke in his hand. From it fell some white objects. He poked at them with one finger but did not pick them up. Libby bent over to look closer.

"Teeth!" She was startled.

"Teeth?" Christie echoed. What were teeth doing here?

"Cougar, maybe." Toliver still poked at them. "And that—that's from a deer. I think this must have been a necklace. See? They were all strung on this rotted cord."

"Let's have a look!" Neal crowded in beside him. "Say, that's great. How many are there? Be sure we get them all—we can string them again."

But Toliver made no move to pick them up. Only Neal started grubbing away in the gravel to collect the scattered teeth. A moment later he looked up wonderingly at the Navajo boy. "Hey, don't you want these?"

"No." Toliver stood up and walked back a pace or two. "They are medicine things."

"Medicine things?" Christie asked. "You

mean like pills or measle shots? How can teeth be medicine? You swallow those and they would hurt your stomach."

"The Old Ones"—Toliver had a strange look on his face now—"they believed differently from the way we do. They had things they thought gave them power—good luck. If a warrior killed a cougar, then he might wear its teeth. He felt he was stronger, like some of the animal's power was now in him. It was a sign of his bravery, but also of the cougar's courage and cunning. When a man went on the war trail, he wore necklaces like this one to make him braver."

"Yeah." Neal sat back on his heels, still holding the teeth he had gathered. "I read about that. Indian boys went out by themselves to have dreams. They weren't allowed to eat until they dreamed about something—an animal, maybe. Then this animal was to help them somehow."

"Some tribes did that, yes. Others had different ways," Toliver answered. "But a necklace such as this—it was truly a medicine thing."

Neal juggled the teeth from one hand to the other. Christie could tell that he wanted them very much. Then he glanced up at Toliver, who stood there quietly as if he were waiting for something important to happen. Neal got to his feet quickly and walked over to where there was a deep bank of sand. Scooping a hole in that, he dropped the teeth in and covered them over with a sweep of his fingers.

He did not say anything, nor did any of the others. They just went back to picking over the gravel and soon found two more arrowheads. To his delight Parky chanced on a well-shaped whole one. Then Perks asked for a drink and said she was hungry. So they went back to where they had left the picnic basket in a small shaded pocket. Baron had given up trying to frighten the chuckawalla out of hiding and had gone off exploring, once sending a bird squawking angrily out of a hole in a saguaro.

Shan was lying in the shade, watching the dog lazily as if he knew Baron was never going to catch anything interesting. Christie fastened the cat's leash to a rock and put out food and water for him.

It was getting a lot hotter and she began to feel as if she did not want to go back and grub in the sand. Then Baron started barking very loudly and urgently once more, and Parky and Perks ran to see what he was after. Christie, mindful of needing to watch them, followed reluctantly.

The big dog was circling around a huge untidy mass on the ground, a mound almost as tall as Christie herself. It looked like a rubbish heap. There were pieces of dried cactus, bits of bleached wood, some twisted strings that might have been leather that had laid out in the open a long time, hunks of withered grass. Scattered all over it were spikes of cactus, as if set there on purpose to warn off any investigation.

"Wood rat nest," Libby explained as she joined Christie. "They carry off all kinds of things to build it. Look here—" She stooped to pull at an end of rag caught on one of the thorns. It came apart as had the old thong Toliver had found. "That's real old."

"But there's a tin can," Christie pointed. "Where would they find that?"

"Hunter's camp, maybe, or they could even have brought it all the way from the station. No use you making such a noise," Libby told Baron. "Old man rat isn't going to come out and say howdy to you!"

"Don't touch anything," Christie warned the twins. "See all those thorns? Get those in your fingers and they would really hurt."

"Rat knows that," Libby laughed. "It's his way of keeping the roof on his house."

"What's this?" Christie had started to turn away when she caught sight of something entangled in the mess. She leaned over and picked at it carefully, trying hard to avoid the spines. But when she tried to tug free what she held, she discovered that the rest must be deeply embedded in the nest. It looked like leather, perhaps part of a belt.

Toliver worked the find loose, suffering stabs

from two thorns in the process. When he straightened it out on the ground, they were all excited.

"Belt and pistol holster!" Neal cried as if he could hardly believe it. "It must be old!"

"Sure is," Toliver agreed. "Guess it's so dry in here that the leather didn't rot. This might even be for a Colt .45. Dad would know. And if that's true you've got yourselves a good show piece for your museum."

Where did it come from? Christie wondered. The station? Or was this a place where there had really been a fight—like those Pinto talked about? She glanced around with a little shiver. A man just wouldn't leave his gun belt unless he had no more use for it—she could guess that much. Suddenly she wanted to go home, but she would not say so.

Neal prowled around the edge of the nest, peering into the mass in search of other treasures. Perks pulled at Christie's hand.

"That's just a dirty old thing!" She kicked at the belt. "Let's go and look for arrowheads again."

"Perks, you stop that!" Neal shouted. "That's a very important find. And, Parky, don't you dare pull at it! Want a cactus spine in your hand? Christie, you get those kids out of here before they get into trouble."

"Come on Parky, Perks." She was willing enough. "Let's go hunt arrowheads."

Perhaps Parky had been cowed by Neal's shout, because he did come. She took both children back to the gravel bed, but it was so hot she did not see how they could stay. Libby sat down with her back to the wall in what shade there was and Christie joined her. A few minutes later the twins flopped down beside them.

Christie felt sleepy. Perks, curled up with her head on Christie's lap, dozed off. I'll just close my eyes for a minute, the older girl thought. It is so quiet—just for a minute—

"Chris! Please, Chris—" Her head jerked and she opened her eyes, not quite sure for a moment where she was. The shadows had crept out farther, but beyond them the sunlight was still bright enough to make her blink.

"Chris! Please, Chris, wake up!" Perks was pulling at her shoulder.

She came fully awake, for there were tear streaks down Perks' round cheeks, cutting tracks through the dust.

"Perks!" She threw her arm about the small girl. "Perks, honey, what's the matter? Are you hurt?"

Perks smeared one hand across her eyes. More tears spilled over. "Chris—Shan—he's lost! We hunted 'n' hunted—but he's lost!"

Shan! How—and where? Christie scrambled up, still holding on to the crying Perks. She saw Libby was standing, too, looking about her.

"What's the matter?" asked the Navajo girl.

"Shan. Perks says he's gone. But how—"

Surely before she had settled down by the rocks she had fastened Shan's leash back on the handle of the picnic basket—she distinctly remembered doing that. The cat might have been able to drag the basket along if he pulled hard enough, but he could not have gone far with that as an anchor. It was the way they always left him when they went on a picnic.

"I'm sure I fastened his leash to the basket—"

"You did. I saw you," Libby assured her.

"Maybe his harness got open. But it was buckled— Or the leash could have broken—"

"Parky was hungry," Perks jerked out between sobs. "He wanted a cookie and he had to take the leash off to get the basket open."

"But Perks, then you should have put the leash over a rock—like I did at noon!"

"We—we forgot!" Perks's sobs turned into a loud wail.

"What's going on?" Neal tramped up to the picnic basket just as Christie arrived from the other direction. He was smudged and dirty and looked hot and tired.

"Shan's gone," Christie told him. "The twins wanted cookies and took his leash off the basket to get them."

"I told her, I told her, I told her!" Parky scrambled over a rock into sight. "I said 'Perks, put Shan's leash on the rock.' And she forgot—"

Perks let out another wail and burrowed her face against Christie.

"You opened the basket, Parky. *You* should have put the leash on the rock," Christie snapped, and then gathered Perks to her closely. "Perks, honey, don't cry so. You know Shan doesn't like strange places. Now let's all be quiet while I call him. You'll see him come because he's probably almost as frightened as you are. But you'll have to be quiet so Shan can hear."

"I'll try," Perks said in a small, muffled voice.

"Shan—Shan—here, boy. Shan!" Christie tried to make her voice firm yet coaxing. It was true that Shan would come when she called, but only if he chose to. And he might not be as frightened at finding himself loose as she had assured Perks. If he were curious and had gone exploring, he could be anywhere.

Shan did not come, nor did he reply to her calls as he sometimes did with a little sound that meant, "I'm busy. Don't bother me."

Parky was beginning to sniff now, too. He brushed angrily at his eyes, not wanting to show he shared his twin's despair. Finally Christie left Perks with Libby and made a circuit of the open space, calling, listening, then calling again. Toliver, Libby, and Neal stayed where they were because Christie thought with too many searchers Shan might take cover and not come out at all.

She met Neal at last by the rocks through which they had come.

"He might have gone back." She spoke aloud what she most feared. If Shan was here, hiding somewhere, they had a chance of finding him. However, if he had gone back toward the meadow he could be anywhere and they might never see him again. Christie thought of snakes and coyotes for whom Shan might make a good dinner. In spite of the sun hot on her head and shoulders she felt very cold inside.

Neal caught her sleeve. "We can try Baron!"

Would Baron understand what they wanted him to do? Christie was not sure, and she did not have much hope. Neal whistled for the dog, who came in a rush. The boy caught him on either side of the head, looked down into his eyes, and spoke slowly and distinctly, as if the dog could indeed understand every word.

"Shan, Baron, fetch Shan." With his fingers hooked in the dog's collar he led him over to where Shan had lain in the shade and pushed his head down so he could sniff the stone there. "Fetch, Baron—fetch Shan!"

Neal released his hold and stood back. Baron had been sniffing the rock. Suddenly Christie felt a little more hopeful. If Baron could trail Shan—

Shan must still have his leash on. Suppose that had become caught, was holding him prisoner somewhere so he couldn't come? Baron still sniffed, then he raised his head and looked at Neal as if wondering what to do next.

"Find Shan—find!" Neal ordered sharply.

The dog gave one more sniff and did move away, nose close to the ground as if he were following a scent! Christie held her breath. Baron was heading for their back trail. Oh, if Shan had gone into the open could even Baron trail him there? The dog moved slowly, stopping many times to sniff. Because they had no other hope, the children followed him.

4
Shan the Explorer

Baron continued to move slowly, stopping now and then for a long sniff at some rock. Christie twisted her hands together. They could not even be sure the dog was trailing Shan—he could be after a rabbit or one of those chuckawalla things. Suppose Shan had gone in the opposite direction and was caught now by leash or harness—maybe choking!

The dog came to a big slide of rock and poked his nose between two boulders. Then he gave an excited bark and began to dig, showering gravel and sand over the children, who were crowding closer. Neal caught him by the collar and pulled him back while Toliver squatted down, his head so low that he, too, might have been smelling out a trail.

"There's a hole back here," he reported. He

pushed tighter against the rocks and shoved his hand and then his arm into the crevice. "Goes in pretty far," he reported. "I can't feel any-thing—"

"Let me!" Christie jerked at his shoulder. "If Shan *is* in there maybe he'll come when I call."

She crouched down in Toliver's place. "Shan! Shan!" she cried, with her mouth as close to that hole as she could get it.

Then they listened, so they *could* hear the thin, hollow-sounding wail that answered her. It was one Shan always used when in trouble.

"He can't get out!" Christie was as sure of that as if she could see. "Maybe his leash is caught somewhere. Oh, Neal, what if we can't get to him!" She shivered.

"Look here!" Toliver's sharpness caught all their attention. He stood a little back, studying the pile of rocks. "I don't think this was just a rock fall. This was built on purpose. Maybe it's a cave someone walled up."

"The Old Ones!" Libby shrank back. "One of their places."

But that did not mean anything to Christie. "If the rocks were put there, then can't we take them away—let Shan out? We *have* to!"

"Stand back, Christie." Neal had gone to stand beside Toliver. "Maybe if we try taking stones out at the top we can get enough free so someone can crawl through."

"Oh, Neal, we have to, we do!" Christie reached for one of those upper rocks but Toliver caught her wrist.

"This has to be done slowly," he warned her. "We don't want to start any slide. The hole could be part of a mine digging. Neal 'n' me, we'll pick out the rocks and hand 'em to you girls. You pile them over there where they can't fall back. Ready?"

"Yes, yes! Please hurry!" Christie pushed her glasses higher on her sweating nose and held out her hands for the first stone.

It seemed to her that Toliver was far too slow in picking out the proper rocks, loosening them with such care he was just wasting time. She handed them on to Libby, who laid them on the ground while Parky and Perks rolled them out of the way.

The hole *was* growing larger. Now they could hear more wails from Shan, uttered at intervals as if he wanted them to hurry. A big lizard flashed into view and Baron barked and leaped before Neal could stop him, so that stones tumbled and the hole was nearly covered again.

"Parky," Neal ordered, "you catch Baron and keep him away from here."

Once more Toliver pried at stones, now using the blade of his belt hatchet.

"I don't think this is a mine shaft," he commented.

"The Old Ones," Libby repeated. "Toliver, if this is a place of the Old Ones—"

The Navajo boy paused, continuing to look at the stone on which his hand now rested. "The cat's in there," he said. "The Old Ones would understand why we have to do this."

What did he mean, Christie wondered? That this might be a place where some Indians were—buried? But Shan was in there and that was all that counted.

Toliver passed another rock along, working steadily until a large hole was laid bare. It was so hot, and the dust from their work filled their eyes, noses, and mouths. Christie called to Perks to get a canteen. They drank and then Toliver went back to work. Now there was a hole large enough to wriggle through. Christie crowded forward.

"I'll go."

Neal's arm swung up before her. "I'll go— I've got this." He had his flashlight in his hand.

"Better me." Toliver was all ready to boost himself in.

"No. Shan doesn't know you," Neal said. "It has to be me. Here goes—"

He scrambled up and slid carefully in. Toliver put head and shoulders in after him. Christie heard a hollow noise that sounded like stones rattling down inside. Was Neal going to fall into a big hole?

60

"It's a cave," Toliver reported. "Something back in there—"

"Shan, here, Shan!" Neal's voice sounded queer and hollow. "Shan—no! Let me—got you!" The last was triumphant and Christie gave a sigh of relief.

"Here." A moment later Toliver turned and handed out Shan, spitting and hissing, kicking against such indignity. His fight subsided when Christie's hands closed about him. She spoke to him soothingly and stroked his head, so busy with Shan that she did not notice at first that Neal had not come back out of the hole. When she realized that, she was afraid again. Was Neal now caught in turn?

"Neal?" she asked Toliver, who was back halfway through the hole. "What is he doing in there?"

Toliver muttered something she could not understand and then drew himself out and went to work quickly loosening more stones.

"Is Neal caught in there?" Christie pulled at the Navajo boy's arm.

"No. But he's found something! And—" Toliver glanced back at his sister as if to reassure her—"it's not Old Ones' things either!"

He was excited. Christie carried Shan back to the picnic basket and made very sure he would stay out of trouble by shutting him in it, the lid tied down. Then she hurried back to where Toliver was again pulling out stones and

Libby putting them to one side. It was not long before they had a big opening through which they could all see.

Neal was hidden by shadows, but the light of his flash shone full on a heap in the middle of a small cave. Boxes and bags. What did they hold? One at a time the rest crawled through to inspect the discovery closer.

Christie saw a small trunk and a bag with a handle, looking a little like a plane bag but larger. There were several other bags tied at the top. Toliver picked up a flatter pouch from the floor. He blew dust from it, rubbed it with his hand. Black letters appeared as he loosened that covering. U.S. MAIL.

"But what is it all? And how did it get here?"

"Maybe from a stagecoach." Toliver walked around the find. "They could have dumped all this if they had to make a quick run, maybe because of an Apache raid. Look there—" He reached into the heap and pulled something into the full beam of the torch. "This is a shotgun— a real old one—the kind a stagecoach guard would have."

"If the Apaches were after them, wouldn't they have needed all their guns?" Neal wanted to know.

"Could be they had no more shells for it."

"That mailbag." Neal centered the light full on it. "We ought to give that to the postman.

Isn't there some kind of law about mail having to be handled that way?''

"Letters in there, if there are any," Toliver commented, "have been on the way a good long time. Don't think anyone's still waiting for them now."

"How long has all this been here, do you suppose?" Christie asked.

"Last raid must have been close to a hundred years ago now," Toliver answered.

A *hundred* years! It was hard to think of that trunk, the bags, and all the rest being shut up here for a hundred years. Christie wondered what had happened to the people who had left them there. Toliver said these might have been hidden to lighten a stage load so they could get ahead faster and escape. But nobody ever came back to get them, so— Suddenly she wanted to get out of this dark cave and forget about what might have happened to the people who had been here once.

"Chris!" Neal was excited. "Don't you see—this is just what we need for the Plan! For a museum at the station—things that were carried on the old stagecoaches—better than arrowheads. It's super!"

"But—they don't belong to us. What about the people who left them here?"

"A hundred years ago?" Neal demanded. "Nobody would be alive now. Maybe we'd never be able even to find out who they were.

Listen here—let's just cover this up until we get a chance to come back and really look it over. Dad—Mother—they're too busy to want to be bothered now. We'll come back tomorrow, bring some stuff to wipe all this clean. Maybe we'll even just leave it here in the cave—fix it up a little so people can see it better, then show it off just as we found it. This is the kind of things tourists want to see!"

"Could be you're right," Toliver agreed. "We could pick the rest of the stones out of the opening, make it easier to get in. Maybe take a little of the stuff out, though—the shotgun, the mailbag." It was clear he agreed with Neal about the value of Shan's find.

- However, Christie was still uneasy. Perhaps the people who had owned this *were* dead a long time ago, but— Well, it had been hidden so long it would not hurt to let it stay where it was a little longer. And when Father was not so busy they could ask him about it.

Neal was continuing: "I vote we don't say anything about this until we get it cleaned up—ready to be seen. Then we ask them to come for a big surprise—"

"Okay," Toliver agreed.

Neal turned to the twins, who had been staring round-eyed at the pile of dusty luggage.

"That means you, too—no talking about this! You just show your arrowheads and say we were hunting them. But not this—we want it to be a surprise."

Both of them nodded. "But we get to help unpack," Parky insisted quickly.

"Nobody unpacks a thing," Neal said sharply, "unless we are all here and do it together. Maybe tomorrow we can sort out part of it. Now let's get out of here and put some of those stones back. We don't want to take a chance of anyone else finding it."

Christie guessed it must be late afternoon by now. If they did not get back to the station soon, someone might come hunting them. However, she stood by, handing stones to the boys. At last Neal and Toliver decided they had done enough, and once more it looked like a natural fall of rock with no cave behind it.

In a hurry, Christie released Shan from the picnic basket, while Libby packed what was left of their lunch. Then they started the reluctant twins homeward, leaving the boys behind to give the last touches to the rocks hiding their find.

The Navajos who had come to help at the station were camping out near the Wildhorse van, and they had already started a cooking fire when the children came across the meadow. Christie discovered, to her relief, that Mother was just beginning to wonder about them. She listened to Parky's tale of arrowheads and said she was glad they had such a good time. When

Christie ventured to suggest they might picnic again tomorrow, Mother seemed relieved and agreed at once—anything, their sister thought, to keep the twins out from underfoot.

It was after the twins had gone to bed that Neal signaled Christie and they slipped out of the room where Mother and Father were talking to Mr. Wainwright, the contractor from town.

"You're not planning to go back to the cave tonight!" Christie had a sudden suspicion.

"'Course not! I want to talk to Pinto. Maybe he can give us some idea why those things were left there."

"You are going to tell him? But I thought it was to be a secret."

"Not tell him, no. Just ask about the times when there were those raids here. Could be he knows some story to explain about the things being hid."

Pinto was sitting on the broad sill of the shed he claimed as his own quarters. As the children came up, he shook flakes of tobacco into a piece of paper, which he rolled into a crumpled-looking cigarette. Christie had never seen that done before.

"Do you always make your own cigarettes?"

"Sure do. Old trick for range hands. I ain't learned many new ones. See here—" He showed her the little drawstring-tied bag of tobacco and a packet of papers. "These here are what we used to call 'the makin's.' There weren't store-bought cigarettes then. A man made his own or chawed or went without. So you was off grubbin' for Injun things today. Find much?"

"Some arrowheads and part of a spearhead," Neal answered. "Toliver found a necklace of teeth. The string fell apart when he picked it up. He didn't want it—said it might be 'medicine'—like warriors wore into battle to make them brave."

"Medicine." Pinto nodded as if he understood that very well. "Depended a lot on their 'medicine,' they did. Sometimes when they got to thinkin' their 'medicine' wasn't good, they'd stop right in the middle of a fight and light out."

"Pinto," Neal said, "you talked about Apaches attacking the station. Did they do that often?"

"Often enough to keep a man on his toes wonderin' when it was goin' to happen agin. Station was changed some from the way you see it now. Your pa, he's plannin' to turn it back a little—make it more interestin' to them tourists. It used to be more like a real fort. Them walls that's now only stones and 'dobe lyin' around—they was built up. The main buildin', it was alongside of one wall, this here bunkhouse and smithy against th'other side. There was some buildin's over there—that's where teamsters an' travelers not comin' by stage could fort up if there was a bad raid. Kept four, five men on guard here all the time. They'd put the horse an' mules in the center to be safe. There was just one gate to let in the stage and team. An' they kept lookout posts up the road a ways.

"They was lucky here because of the spring. Station built around that so had water all the time. For a while—while Manico, the Apache War chief, was raidin'—they kept an army patrol here, too."

"Were you here then, Pinto?"

"Well, boy, I may be old, but I ain't got that many years behind me. M'pa was, though, and I heard him tell 'bout those times. You see, before pa was a young'un and came to this country it was boomin'—mines gettin' out gold and silver, the army ridin' herd on the 'Paches and tryin' to keep peace. Then came the War Between the States—what folks call the Civil War now. The army pulled out and went back east to do their fightin'. Then the 'Paches, they took it into their heads that it was them who beat and scared the army home. So they just cut loose, and in this whole country there weren't hardly anyplace a white man dared rest easy. Pete Kitchen down Tubac way—he had a regular fort built on his ranch and he held out. Got the Pimas on his side. They hated 'Paches and fought for him.

"But otherwise there weren't no Arizona,

nor not much of New Mexico neither, safe for white skins. The stage people, who was here then, they had to give in and clear out. Went broke, that first stage line did. And the mines—men walked off and left 'em. That was a bad time.

"Then the war back east finished and the army came back. Only the 'Paches, they were so sure they licked the whites first time around, they weren't goin' to give up easily. The miners, they was itchin' to get back to what they had had to leave. So there were all kinds of little wars as went on, with the army ridin' themselves weary tryin' to get things back into shape.

"Sam Bright, he was the man who started the stage goin' this way again, back in '67 that were. There were good, rich strikes back in the hills, plenty of them—gold comin' out, men goin' in. He went around hirin' his people outta the war back east. They might not know Injuns too good—though some of 'em being scouts before the war did—but they was good shots. Had him a sort of private army, Bright did. He built three, four stations like this one. Others he took over from the first companies—put his men in. Then he began runnin' the line. Sometimes he had more guards than passengers. But he didn't lose many coaches and he got a rep like Pete Kitchen for holdin' out and being tough enough to make the 'Paches think twice.

"Then he made a treaty for hisself with some of the Navajos and they took to doin' his scoutin'—just like the Pimas did for Kitchen. This station was important in those days. I seen, when I was a real little tad, a colonel sittin' down here with Bright and some Navajos talkin' things out. 'Course that was nigh to the end of all the trouble. The 'Paches, they got crowded out and had to go on reservations. Then Bright had nothin' but some road agents now and then to worry 'bout."

"What were road agents?" Christie wanted to know.

"Thieves—after the strongboxes."

Strongboxes—Christie remembered TV shows she had seen. Gold dust coming from the mountain mines. Why, there might be even some among those things they had found today! Could it belong to them because they had found it?

"Then the mines began to peter out," Pinto went on. "Stage came through maybe once a month, not twice a week like before. Darringer closed down. Maybe just one or two old desert rats still bunked out there doin' some pannin' and a little hammerin' around. The town died and so did the stage line. Only Bright had made this station such a good, tight place it lasted longer than them what had used it."

"When the Indians attacked, the people who were traveling just stayed in the station, didn't

71

they? They didn't try to get away?'' Neal wanted to know.

"They weren't stupid,'' Pinto said. "Who'd get out from behind walls and try to make a run for it with maybe a 'Pache behind every rock waitin' to cut 'em down. The 'Paches, they didn't go chargin' around on horses like the other Injuns. They liked to shoot without gettin' shot at—spend a whole day creepin' to pick off a man without him knowin' they were within miles.''

He puffed his twisted cigarette. " 'Course there was always some greenhorns as thought they knew more'n the men who had been here most of their lives. There was a story m'pa told 'bout a couple of dudes—they were from San Francisco—offered a driver big money to make a run out of here when they had to hole up some days. Iffen Bright or one of his head men had been here, he'd have locked 'em up in a hurry, for their own good. M'pa was here, only he had the fever and he was outta his head mosta the time, till it was too late.

"It looked like the 'Paches had beat it. A scout said the only sign he saw was two, three days old. Well, these dudes kept uppin' the price—they was in a tearin' hurry to get away for some reason. Finally they found a stupid wrangler who was only a part-time driver. He said he knew a way up the canyon as might get them out. So they was on to him, wavin' their money in their fists. He knocked out the regular driver and took 'em—and that was the end of 'em all.''

"They never found them, the stage, or discovered anything about what happened?" Neal wanted to know.

"That's the way the story goes. And what made it worse—the 'Paches came in twice as hard in the mornin'. There was one time the station was nearly took. Only a patrol of horse soldiers comin' in drove them off. But it's a story there was no proof of. I'm reckonin' them dudes didn't get very far. Yes, this here station has sure seen some stirrin' times in the old days. Now"—Pinto rose and stretched— "seein' as how I have me a full day of fetchin' and carryin' comin' up tomorrow, I'm goin' to get me a little shut-eye."

"Thank you," Christie said, "for telling us about the station. Good night."

"Good night," Neal echoed her.

As they started back toward the big house, Christie asked in a low voice, "Do you suppose what we found was from that stage? But why put those things in a cave, not just leave them there when they left?"

"They might have started out with them on board and then thought they could make better time without them," Neal answered thoughtfully. "They could have beat it out of here fast,

73

thinking someone would stop them—and then ditched the stuff.''

Christie looked carefully around. A big moon was rising to light the yard and the piles of lumber and materials that had been brought out from town. But there were dark shadows, too. No stagecoach, though, waiting for foolish men to take out into that farther dark where the silent enemy could be waiting. What was the truth behind Pinto's story?

5
Lady Maude

It was quite early when the pounding and noise began the next morning. Christie hurried to help Mother get breakfast. Some of the workers, rather than make the rough trip into town and back every day, were camping out, and they ate with the family. Others had brought their own supplies as had the Navajos. Neal, carrying in what seemed endless armloads of wood pieces to feed the stove, nudged his sister as he passed.

"Did you ask her yet—about our going?"

"Yes, last night. But didn't you hear what Pinto said to Father? It may be going to rain."

"What would that matter? It's dry in the cave."

"But Mother doesn't know about the cave.

She'd think we were going to be out in the open," Christie pointed out.

"All right, I'll ask her again if you won't!" Neal was impatient.

That was not fair, Christie thought, as she set down a tray of used coffee mugs.

"Chris." Perks pulled at her belt from behind. "Chris, when are we going to go—you-know-where?"

"You-know-where?" Mother brought a steaming tea kettle from the stove. "I do hope we can get the water heater in soon. Where is you-know-where, Perks?"

"She means the place where we found the arrowheads," Neal cut in quickly.

"If it rains you won't be going anywhere, Perks, much as I would like you to," Mother answered. "I shall have to drive into town again with Marina to the launderette, or we won't have anything to wear in another day. You and Parky can come along with us, Perks."

"No!" Perks could be as stubborn as Parky when she wished.

"Perks!" Mother's voice was a warning.

"I want to go with Chris and Neal—to that place where all the things are—the dark place—"

"What dark place?"

Neal caught at Perks's shoulder. Christie knew he longed to give the little girl a warning shake and did not quite dare, not with Mother watching.

It was then that Christie was inspired to tell a portion of the truth. "We found a cave," she began. Neal glared at her but she continued anyway. "It has some—"

"Oh, the arrowheads were in a cave? But Christie, caves can be dangerous places. You mustn't go back there alone."

She must have been crazy, Christie thought now.

Neal added swiftly: "This one's all right, Mother. Toliver knows a lot about such things. He's been at that place before—so has Libby."

"I don't know about your going back there— at least not until your father sees it."

Neal shot a very hot look at Christie, which she knew she deserved. If Mother said no now they would have to tell about their discovery. Then maybe (Christie remembered the mailbag) Mother and Father would decide they could not keep the things, and their plan would be spoiled. If they only had time to get to the cave and lay things out, perhaps everyone would be so impressed they would agree to keep them!

"Mother," Neal repeated anxiously, "Toliver has been there, and it really is safe. He's awfully careful about things like that."

"Perhaps—you and Chris—but I don't know about Perks and Parky—"

"Yes, yes, yes!" Perks's voice rose higher

with every yes. One minute more and Mother would say no just because Perks was being so stubborn.

"It really *is* safe there, Mother," Christie assured her. "If you go to the launderette, you're going to be very busy. And the men will be here, too." No need to point out that Perks and Parky could be nuisances at either place if they set their minds to it. Mother already knew that. Mother still wore a frown line. "I want a promise, Christie."

"Yes!" At that moment Christie was ready to promise anything.

"If you go, you'll stay with the twins all the time. And Perks—"

"Yes?"

"You and Parky must promise to mind what Chris and Neal tell you to do, or you won't go back again. Understand? I mean you especially, Parky." The other twin had come up, dragging the picnic basket as if ready to pack it all by himself.

"I promise!" Perks cried, and Christie hoped she meant it.

But Parky was not so sure. "Do I have to just tag along?" His lip stuck out stubbornly.

"If you go at all, you do." Mother was firm.

Parky sighed. "When do we get big enough so's Chris and Neal don't have to look out for us? I get awfully tired of being looked after."

"The sooner you are 'looked after' without

whining and making trouble for Christie and Neal, the closer you are to looking after yourselves," Mother answered tartly. "All right, you can go. But be home earlier than you were last night. And if it rains, keep under cover and get back as soon as you can."

Parky banged the basket down before Christie. "Hurry and get some sandwiches and things! We gotta get there quick!"

Mother laughed. "And you think you need plenty of sandwiches and things, Parky? Well, get me the peanut butter, Christie—and the jelly—"

" 'N cookies and bananas," chanted Parky.

"There are no more bananas and not many cookies." Mother set the basket down on top of the long table. "If you people are going to go picknicking every day we shall have to lay in more of that kind of supplies. As it is, Parky, you'll have to do with what we have left for today."

Parky stood on one leg and hopped. "I'm going outside. Come on, Perks. And we don't want to wait too long."

Christie opened jars and got sandwich bags ready. But Mother did not begin spreading bread at once. Instead she looked from Christie to Neal.

"I told the twins that you two are in charge, and I mean it. But also, don't order them around. You know that only makes Parky stubborn. And Perks follows his lead in everything. So both of *you* watch what you say and don't start trouble. If it weren't that the washing has to be done and the twins hate waiting at the launderette, I wouldn't leave them. Just you be careful.''

"Yes, Mother," Christie answered, and Neal nodded.

The basket was filled at last and Christie put Shan on his leash. She was going to be extra careful about him today. Letting Neal carry the basket, she cuddled the cat in her arms. The twins were waiting outside with Baron.

As they passed the old bunkhouse Pinto called to them: "Rain comin'. You watch out—don't go too far."

"We found a cave," Parky answered. "Rain can't get at us if we go in that."

"A cave?" Pinto sounded surprised. "First time I heard tell of a cave 'round here. When I get me a little more time I'll mosey over and take a look at that. Me, I lived 'round here off 'n' on for a good many years, and this is the first time I heard tell of any cave—"

"Shut up!" Neal said in a fierce whisper to Parky as Christie smiled at the old man.

"It isn't a very big one." She tried quickly to think of something to say that would make their find appear to be of little importance. "We're going to look for arrowheads—"

"Toliver and Libby goin' with you? It's better if they do—they've enough sense to know what kind of shelter to find. Good luck huntin'."

"Thanks!" Neal used the basket to bump the twins on ahead. "We told you," he was hissing as Christie caught up, "that the cave's got to be a secret for now. Then you, Perks, and you Parky, have to go blabbin' it all around!"

"Christie told Mother!" Perks exploded indignantly. "She did! I heard her."

"Only after you had started talking too much yourself." With that Neal made Christie feel better. "Now, if you're going to help with the Plan, you've got to keep quiet until we're ready. Maybe if other people knew now they wouldn't let us keep that stuff."

"Maybe we can't anyway," Christie said in a low voice. "Once they see it. That mailbag, Neal—shouldn't we bring that home and give it to the postman?"

"Why? It's so old now the letters in it—if there *is* anything in the bag—won't mean much. They'd only go to the dead letter office probably."

Parky was surprised. "What's a dead letter office?" he demanded.

"We learned about that in social studies last year," Neal answered. "Letters that can't be delivered, when there's no return addresses on them, are sent there. They open them up to find if there is anything inside to tell who sent them or who they are for. If they can't find out, then that's that—they throw them out. The people those letters were written to—those in the bag—must all be dead, too. So I don't see why we couldn't have them to show—they wouldn't be any use to anyone."

Neal sounded reasonable, but Christie had an idea that Mother and Father, and maybe the mailman, might not agree. But they did not have to decide just yet.

"I wonder why the people who left all the stuff never came back to get it," Perks said. "And why was it put there anyway?"

Could all those things have come out of the coach Pinto had told them about—the one that had tried to get through the attackers? Perhaps they never really would know.

But Neal was more optimistic: "Maybe we can find out. But we have to get going now. Hey, there's Toliver and Libby!"

The Navajos came hurrying to meet them.

"Thought perhaps you couldn't come today," Toliver said. "It's going to rain, so we'd better hurry to get to the cave before the storm catches us. Look what I have." He held out two camp lanterns. "Just put fresh batteries in these and they'll last a good long time. We need more than just a flashlight in there now."

Libby carried a bag slung over her shoulder. "I brought some extra lunch. Here, wait a minute." She paused by a big bush and, taking out a knife like Toliver's, sawed off a heavy branch thick with leaves, which she handed to Christie before cutting another for herself. "We can use these to sweep out the dust."

The girls had lagged behind and by the time they caught up the boys were already fast at work unpacking the stones they had used to conceal the entrance. Neal started to throw them out helter-skelter in his haste to get in until Toliver pointed out they would be needed again and started to pile them to one side.

With the camp lanterns on, the cave was brightly lighted, and they could see everything within clearly. There was not too much in the pile after all—two trunks, small and covered with dusty hide, one with tacks pounded in the lid to make the initials C.K., which they could see after Christie and Libby used the branches to sweep them off.

"One thing," Toliver said. "It's been dry in here, so things inside these ought to be in good shape. I wonder—did that holster and belt we found come from here? Maybe the rats found it and dragged it out, or it could have been dropped by one of the men who left this. Now, let's pull these trunks away from each other so we'll have more room to open them up. Which one are we going to do first?"

"This one!" Neal's voice was sharp with excitement. "This is the strongbox! It's got to be. And it's locked!" He was on his knees, tugging vainly at the lid. "Maybe there's gold dust inside."

As he tugged at the box it grated across the stone floor. Grabbing the leafy brush from Christie, he swiped back and forth, sending dust flying to make them all sneeze and draw back a little.

" 'Bright Stage Line,' " Neal read, running a grimy finger over the lettering. "This sure *must* be the strongbox! But how are we going to get it open?" He jerked impatiently at the rusty padlock.

"Try hammering it with a stone," suggested Toliver.

What did gold dust look like, Christie wondered—like glittery powder? And how could you turn it into real money? Did you just take it into a bank and say "I want some dollar bills for this"? Did they then weigh it—

Neal had hurried outside to find a suitable rock and was already back, pounding away at the lock without any results. Toliver came back with another and started in to help. But though they battered it, they could not get the thing open.

"No use." Toliver settled back on his heels. "We'll have to have a tire lever or something like that to bust this. Have to wait to do it."

Neal, red-faced from his efforts, looked very disappointed. But it was plain they could not force the lock with just stones. "Okay," he said reluctantly, and helped Toliver to drag it to one side.

"Here's another box." Parky tugged aside a very dusty bag. "Say, it looks a lot like that other one and it's got no lock!"

"Let's see!" Neal elbowed Parky aside and jerked what had sat behind the bag into the full light.

It was another metal box, even larger than the strongbox. And when he brushed off the dust there was white lettering on the top. Christie leaned closer to read that. This was not the name of the stage line. Instead it seemed to be an address—very clear now that the dust had been brushed away.

" 'Miss Maude Woodbridge, Woburnscott, Maine. Handle with care.' " Neal read aloud. "This must have been important, all done up like this. But there's no lock, how did they keep it shut?"

Toliver moved one of the lanterns a little closer. "It's been sealed. See here?" There were rope handles on either side by which to carry it, but all around the edge of the lid ran a red line. He pushed at it with a fingernail. "Old waxy stuff, real dry now—it ought to be easy to break." Unsheathing his knife, he began to pick at the strip and the dull red stuff came away in flakes.

Even with the sealing all gone, they had to pry, Toliver with his knife, Neal using one of the stones as a clumsy lever. Then Toliver held up the lamp as the lid finally came off.

"Newspapers! Just a lot of old newspapers!" Neal cried out in disappointment, and would have jerked at them roughly had not Libby caught his arm.

"Those are very old papers. Look and see what the date on them is."

"Eighteen seventy-five." He held the lantern very close to the print. "The *London Times*—but that's an English newspaper!"

"Libby's right—they may be worth something, being so old," Christie pointed out. "We have to be careful. Old English newspapers found way out here—that's strange enough for any museum! Take them out carefully—they may fall apart, they're so old."

Neal looked down at his dirty hands. "Maybe you girls better do it—we're too dirty."

The layers of paper were so brittle that, in spite of all their efforts to be careful, a lot just fell apart. But it was a very thick layer and some in the middle were better preserved. Under all those sheets was folded cloth, yellowish and queer-smelling. Lying on that was an envelope.

"Miss Maude Woodbridge" was written on it. Christie picked it up with the same care with which she had handled the papers. It was not sealed, as she could see when she turned it over. After a moment of hesitation she drew out the folded paper it contained.

"It's a letter. Perhaps we shouldn't read it—you should never read other people's mail."

"It's a dead letter, just like Neal said," Parky spoke up. "Neal says they open and read dead letters. So you can do it, Christie."

She held the brown-edged paper into the full light of the nearest lamp. The writing was very clear, though there were queer fancy flourishes to make it different from any she had ever seen before.

My dear little daughter:

The Sea Maid made a record voyage to San Francisco. But there I found disturbing news awaiting me. I shall not be able to return home as I had promised. The Sea Witch was here in port lacking a master, Captain Daniels having died of the fever. The Sea Maid, as I told you in my last letter, is being sold to a South American company, but the Sea Witch has a full cargo for Hong Kong and I must take her there.

Thus I shall not spend your birthday at home with you this year as we have both so longed would be.

Mr. Hawkins, the mate of the Sea Maid, intends to return east overland, carrying some important papers for the company.

He has kindly consented to take Lady Maude in his charge. I know that she will not be the same as having your father with you, but I think you shall find her a charming addition to your family.

She comes from Paris, France. But in a very roundabout way, for I found her in Hong Kong. She had been sent there for another little girl's birthday gift but arrived too late, for a sudden change in Mr. Lebrebre's plans had already taken him and his family out of the city and on their way back to France. So, since Mr. Lebrebre's replacement had no use for her, he was willing to let me buy her. Thus, when she reaches you, she will have traveled almost around the world!

All her clothes and belongings accompany her and I think you will discover that she is a very fine lady indeed. I shall write you again as soon as I have time. And may we be together before Christmas. I shall pray that is so, and so you do likewise.

Your loving father,
Asa Woodbridge, Captain

"Lady Maude," repeated Neal blankly. "But she—"

"Let me." Christie pushed him aside, tucking the letter, once again in its envelope, inside her shirt.

88

She drew out the cloth. The odor from the box grew stronger—it was a very pleasant one. Christie sniffed at the folds of the material. Yes, that was where it was coming from.

"Smells good!" Perks caught at the edge of the cloth and held it to her nose. "Nice, like Nana's old fan—"

"Sandalwood!" Christie now remembered her grandmother's carved fan, too.

Under the sweet-smelling cloth was a bundle wrapped around and around in more cloth. The edges of that were fastened with dabs of red sealing wax.

"Here, let me."

As Christie held the bundle, Toliver carefully pried at the seals with the point of his knife until they broke so that Christie could unwind the wrapping. As that finally fell away Neal took one astounded look and then gave a disgusted snort: "Nothing but just an old doll! What's all the fuss about that?"

6
Trouble at Ten Mile

"Not just a big old doll!" protested Christie, being very careful how she drew away the cloth that had been sealed for so long. "This is"—she tried to remember the right words—"a French fashion doll!"

"So what's the difference?" Neal wanted to know.

"Remember when Mother and I went to the doll show at the auditorium last year—the one where all the collectors showed their old, old dolls? They even had a piece about it in the paper."

"I remember, if Neal doesn't!" Perks cried. "I went, too!"

"Mrs. Edwards, the lady from the church who sold Mother our tickets, showed us some of the dolls she said were worth a lot of money.

There was one something like this, dressed just like a lady of a long time ago.''

"She even had a little umbrella," Perks broke in again.

"Mrs. Edwards called it a parasol," Christie corrected.

"And a fan, and little gloves, and a purse, and real earrings in her ears." Perks turned her description into a kind of chant. "Only we couldn't touch her—they had her standing up in a big glass case."

"That for sure—that dolls like this are worth a lot of money?" Toliver stooped for a closer look. "Hey, this one's wearing earrings, too. And a necklace—"

"I think that's a watch chain. See? The end of it's tucked into her belt. Ladies wore watches like that once." Christie held the doll upright, folding the cloth about her to keep it between her own dirty hands and the flounced and ruffled dress.

"Lady Maude," Libby said. "That's the right name for her, isn't it? She looks proud and important—like she's somebody."

Lady Maude had puffs and curls of dark red hair, brown eyes, and lashes and brows of what Christie thought might be real hair, too—not just painted on. On the elaborate rolls and curls of hair perched a small hat with curled black plumes. The earrings that had been fitted into very tiny holes in her ears looked gold and

showed sparks of red stones. Her dress, with all its stiff ruffles and drapings, was dark green, her small boots black. And she did have gloves on, while a swinging metal purse, very small, was clipped to the belt of her dress. Around her shoulders was a black velvet cape lined in fur, and a small muff of the same fur had been fitted over one of her hands.

"There's more in there." Neal pointed into the box. "Let's see what it is!" He tried to reach over Christie's shoulder.

"Be careful! Don't you dare touch anything with those dirty hands!" she commanded. "Libby, you hold Lady Maude." She passed the doll to the Navajo girl and lifted up another layer of packing. Again the sweet sandalwood smell was strong. What lay beneath were Lady Maude's belongings.

There was a good-sized (for a doll) trunk with a high, rounded top. It was covered with leather and had a small gold-painted crown on the lid with *M* below. With that were two round hat boxes, also doll size, two bags made of brightly colored flowered material like carpet, a parasol, and a second, smaller trunk. Christie bounced she was so excited.

"She has clothes, a lot of clothes!"

"Nothing more?" Neal was plainly disappointed. "Just doll clothes. Let's open something else." He turned away to inspect the rest of the boxes and bags.

Christie paid no attention to him but rather spoke to Libby. "If we washed our hands maybe we dare look at the rest."

Libby nodded, as eager as Christie. "Let's just take all this outside!"

Christie was willing to leave the rest to the boys. Lady Maude was too wonderful to just put aside all at once. She picked up the box by its rope handles. It was heavy, but she could manage. Libby carried Lady Maude and Perks tagged along.

Hunting up one of the canteens and a roll of paper toweling, Christie washed her hands and Perks then took the doll while Libby did the same.

Sometime later they sat just staring at a wealth of treasures. Christie had thought that the doll Mrs. Edwards had shown them had lovely things, but Lady Maude was wealthier. There was even a jewel case, holding two more pairs of earrings, a necklace, three bracelets, and a little crown thing to wear in the hair, as well as two jeweled pins. There were stockings folded into a case, shoes, hats, a corset, dressing gown, nightgown, comb, brush, mirror, a very tiny bottle, which must have been meant for perfume, and hairpins so small Christie was afraid they would be lost. Another purse held foreign-looking coins, French maybe, and was laid away among dresses and petticoats all embroidered, tucked, and ruffled—even a pair of eyeglasses mounted on a stick fastened to a chain. And there were long gloves and short ones, all made to fit over the doll's kid hands, which were so perfectly made that even the tiny fingers were separated by sewing.

"You know, Christie, even in those days, when things were a lot cheaper, Lady Maude must have cost a lot of money." Libby surveyed all they had unpacked as if she could not quite believe what she saw.

"Maybe even hundreds of dollars," Perks said. "Only—she's fun to look at, but you never could play with her, could you? I'd rather have Raggedy Ann."

"I don't think she was ever meant to be played with, not really," Christie answered. "The doll Mrs. Edwards showed us didn't have near as much as this, and her hair wasn't nice anymore the way Lady Maude's is. I'll bet Lady Maude is worth twice as much as that doll! If she were put in a case, why, everybody would want to come and see her!" Christie thought of a big glass case set in the station. Lady Maude would be better than any old arrowheads.

"I bet she was disappointed," she said slowly.

"Who was disappointed?" Libby wanted to know.

"Maude Woodbridge, the little girl Lady

Maude was going to. I wonder what she thought when Lady Maude never got there."

"Maybe she never even knew the doll was coming," Libby suggested. "That letter was in the box, so she never got it either."

"But she would know about it after her father got home," Christie said. "I wonder if he told her all about Lady Maude. If he did she must have been so sorry she was lost. Why, it's over a hundred years ago! Lady Maude has been lost a long time."

"Look—" Libby had glanced up at gathering clouds. "Rain's coming. We'd better get back under cover."

They dared not hurry too fast in repacking everything for fear they might lose some of the tiny things, so the first big drops fell just as Christie closed the box lid on Lady Maude. Now that she had seen it all she felt that she simply could not leave that box in the cave again. But they pulled it back with them out of the beginning storm.

"We didn't find anything else but a lot of old clothes and such stuff," Neal was plainly disappointed.

"Passengers' luggage." Toliver thumped a small trunk. "But people like to look at old clothes—if they're as queer as some of these. They do belong in a museum, I guess. And we have the shotgun, that belt and holster out of the rats' nest—"

"And the strongbox," Parky reminded them. "Maybe it does have gold dust or something like that in it."

Neal looked a little more cheerful. Christie wondered what he had expected to find. There could not be, she was sure, any more such wonderful surprises as Lady Maude.

"There're some pictures. Look here!" Neal snapped open a case. Fitted neatly into sections made to hold them were a number of small boxes. Some were square, some oval, one or two round. Neal pried one out and opened it so the girls could see a framed picture of a woman. She wore clothes like those of Lady Maude and rested her elbow on a pillar so she looked stiff and uncomfortable, as if having one's picture taken hurt.

"All different pictures." Neal snapped the big case shut again. "This was inside with them." He held out a card covered with his own dusty fingerprints.

" 'Hiram Peabody, Representative, Smithers and Son, Supplies for Photography Studios—' "

"These must have been samples—the kind of picture frames people liked then. That's all— just clothes, the strongbox, and the mail sack. Oh, yes, and the doll. We can't keep them here in the cave to show off like we thought—they'd all get too dirty."

"We could have cases—glass ones—in the

station house," suggested Christie. Lady Maude *must* be protected.

"Have to be a lot of cases, maybe. And I don't know about showing off old clothes," Neal answered doubtfully.

"Lady Maude's best! She's wonderful!" Perks cried. "You didn't see—but she has all sorts of things! Little, little hairpins, and hankies, and a bustle—that makes her dress stick out in the back like the ladies' in the olden days—Christie showed me. Anybody would want to see Lady Maude!"

"Yeah? She really comes with all that?" Neal demanded of Christie, showing much more interest.

"More things than I ever thought any doll could—like a Barbie, only the things are all old, as they had then and not now. She's just like the doll Mrs. Edwards said was a 'museum piece'—only better, because she was never handled much or had her things lost. So—we put her in a museum—our very own."

"We'd have to find out about getting a case. And with everybody so busy, maybe we'd better not bother them about it now," Neal said doubtfully.

Leave Lady Maude here! Christie could hardly bear to think of that. But she had been safe for a good many years, so perhaps a few more days would not matter. Mother would be so surprised. Christie wanted so much to show her. She bent over to shove the box farther back against the wall and the letter she put inside her shirt prodded against her. Should she put that back in the box? Or would it be better to take it to the station—maybe show it to Mother?

"I'm hungry." Parky tugged at the fastening on the picnic basket and Shan uttered one of his sharp cries for immediate attention.

Libby brushed a clean space on the floor with one of the leafy branches and Neal and Toliver went to the mouth of the cave to hold their hands out into the now steadily falling rain for a quick wash, herding Parky along to do likewise. The girls opened the basket and the bags the Wildhorses had brought.

"That rain's so thick it looks like a wall," Neal reported, "and there's a big stream running along out there."

"Won't last long," Toliver said as the boys wiped their hands on the paper towels Christie handed around.

When they settled down to eat, they faced out into the rain. As Neal had said, it was now a curtain. Somehow that seemed to make the inside of the cave a big safe room.

"You know"—Toliver licked a bit of mustard from one brown finger—"it's funny Mr. Toner hasn't been around yet to see what's going on at the station."

"Who's Mr. Toner?"

"He's boss over at the ranch, wants the water rights at the spring. Looking at all that rain just going to waste made me think about him. Pinto's had to be tough with old G.T. the past few years. There was something in the law about the station—it couldn't be sold for a long time. Well, Pinto was worried about this year 'cause that law was running out, and he thought G.T. would get it. Must have made him feel good to have you folks arrive. Did your father buy it from the company?"

"Pinto did say something about that." Neal chewed away thoughtfully at a sandwich. "I remember now. But it must be ours now or we wouldn't have moved here."

"How come you wanted to be here anyway?" Toliver asked.

"Well, Dad lost his job in Mayfield. His company was bought out by another firm. And Dad always wanted to live out here. You see, when he was in the army a couple of fellows in his outfit were Navajos. When the war was over he visited them out here, and he liked the country a lot. But there wasn't any sort of job he could do here then. He kept talking about it, showing pictures he took and reading a lot of books.

"Then he heard about them opening the new park and building the highway. He was going to buy a motel, but the down payment was too big. Some real estate man wrote him about this place. He sent Dad pictures and a Mr. Colby who was in the army with Dad was willing to go partners. Dad's to run the station and Mr. Colby is going to manage the publicity—"

"Dad had to borrow a lot of money for it too," Parky suddenly piped up. "He worries about that."

"Parky!" Christie demanded. "How did you—"

"I heard him telling Mom—with my own ears I heard him. So did Perks, didn't you?"

His twin nodded. "He said it was awfully important to get the place ready fast and yet not spend too much. Christie, you said maybe Lady Maude is worth a lot of money. Could we sell her and give the money to Dad, and then maybe he wouldn't worry so much."

"She really isn't ours—yet," Christie answered. "If we could use her to show people, make them want to come to the station to see her, that would help. But she belongs to Maude Woodbridge, not to us, and we'd have to give her back if we were asked."

"That Maude Woodbridge must be dead," Libby said. "Why, she'd be over a hundred! I don't think she'll be asking for Lady Maude, I really don't."

Christie thought about the long time between 1875 and now and felt a little safer. Maybe they could claim Lady Maude. Christie hated to think of selling her. She had so plain in her mind a picture of a big glass case standing at the station house with Lady Maude and all her lovely little things arranged carefully in it. She just knew people would want to see her.

"G.T."—Toliver was back to his own thoughts—"is going to be awfully mad that your father got the station. I don't see how he was able to get it either. G.T. must have had a real estate man all ready to grab it as soon as it was up for sale. He's wanted it for years."

"Maybe he doesn't know anything about it," suggested Libby. "He went east to get Marlene from school, remember? If they were home they'd both be over here by now. Marlene likes to show off her mare."

"You don't like her, do you?" Christie asked.

Libby shrugged. "You don't get to know her enough to either like her or not like her. We're Indians—that's all the Toners know."

Toliver scowled. "Sure. Indians are like some kind of zoo animals as far as the Toners are concerned."

"G.T. called the sheriff once to make us move on when we camped here. Only for once he was wrong." Libby smiled. "Father's second cousin married the sheriff's nephew and Sheriff Wylie himself has a half-Navajo grandmother."

"So Wylie came over in the jeep." Toliver took up the story. "Had him a real solemn face on. G.T. came down to watch us being pushed off. Then Wylie, he looked at the paper Dad carries—it's from the old treaty and it says that any Navajo has the right to stay at the station 'as long as the spring there runs', 'cause they helped out when the Apaches raided. So Wylie tells G.T. that the treaty was signed by the President himself and is law.''

"Then"—Libby's smile grew wider—"Pinto said that G.T. himself was trespassing and wanted the sheriff to warn him off. And Sheriff Wylie said that if the legal caretaker—that's Pinto—registered a complaint, he had to listen. And Pinto told Mr. Toner he *was* trespassing."

"Old G.T. started up his station wagon so fast," Toliver added, "we thought he'd never make the turn out and hit smack into a wall. He just scraped by."

"His face was as red as the cliff. He didn't come back all the time we were here," Libby ended.

"That doesn't mean he'll give up wanting the water rights," Toliver warned. "Perhaps he'll be after your father to sell out to him."

"Dad won't," Neal said confidently. "Hey, the rain's stopped." He stood up. "We can't do any more here until we get something to open the strongbox. No use just sitting around. I vote we go home, come back tomorrow with some tools."

Christie was putting leftovers back in the

basket. She glanced longingly at Lady Maude's box. Shouldn't they take that with them? Now that Toliver had broken through the sealing and they had opened it, perhaps one of those rats might get in, drag off Lady Maude to the big nest. However, when she suggested taking it along, Toliver shook his head.

"The lid's too tight down. Opening it up made the things inside expand. Nothing's going to get in there. We might as well leave it for now. With the rain just over, walking may be kind of hard, water holes and such, and we wouldn't want to drop it into one of those."

Christie had to agree against her will. Shan had gone to the entrance to the cave and was now shaking his forepaws vigorously, one after the other, uttering loudly his dislike of a dripping-wet outer world.

"Here." Libby emptied what remained in her tote back into the Kimballs' basket. She lifted Shan and dropped him into the bag. "You'd better carry him this way. As Toliver said, the walking may be hard and you can manage him better."

Toliver *was* right. The flood of rain had left pools along the floor of the small side canyon. The girls splashed ahead, leaving Neal and Toliver to reseal the cave. At last they had to sit down on still-wet rocks and take off their sandals, roll up their jeans as far as they could, and also see that Parky and Perks were similarly prepared to wade on.

Christie went slowly and carefully. The drifts of sand were soft enough under her feet, but she cried out once when she stepped on a rough piece of gravel.

Libby said quickly, "Look out for cactus bits, Perks, Parky—keep away from those. Give me your hand, Perks. Parky, you go with Christie. We'd better leave the basket here and the boys can carry it. Now—go slow and watch out!"

Twice Libby stopped them all until she could pick up and throw away a spiky piece. Christie was very glad when they were able to squeeze between the entrance rocks and see the meadow ahead.

In spite of rolling up their jeans, those were wet as far as their knees. And it was hard to get their sandals over wet feet to which the sand now stuck like a queer sort of socks. Parky refused to try wearing foot covering until Libby held up a cactus spike right before his eyes.

After the desert the meadow was very green and rain-washed. Susie, Old Timer, and two Navajo horses were grazing as if the fall of water had not bothered them at all, though patches of wet showed on their hides. Christie suddenly remembered what Father had said about washouts on the road when sudden rains came and hoped Mother would not have trouble driving.

"What about the car?" she asked Libby. "Mother and your mother. If they were coming back from town—"

"Washouts? No, I don't think so. This really wasn't a bad storm. You don't need to worry, Christie. It smells clean now, doesn't it?"

Christie, surprised at Libby's question, threw back her head and sniffed. There was a freshness in the air, and she thought she could smell flowers. Shan wriggled and kicked in the bag. His head appeared at the open top and Christie was just in time to prevent his jumping out.

They swished on through the tall grass and passed the Wildhorse van, making for the station house. When they arrived there they discovered that the men were no longer working. Rather they had gathered around looking at a big station wagon. Christie had thought that the Kimball car, meant to carry all of them and camping gear, was large. But this one was even bigger, newer—shiny where the rain had washed off the dust. On the nearest door were big red letters: G. T. RANCH.

"Mr. Toner," Libby said. But there was no one in the driver's seat.

As they came closer, a girl looked at them through the other front window. She had red hair tied back with a bright green ribbon that matched her green shirt. Most of her face was masked by big, dark sunglasses. The glasses had bright green rims, too, which made, Christie thought, their wearer look rather like a grasshopper.

The girl swung open the door and slid out. She also had on pale tan slacks and small, high-heeled riding boots. Facing the girls, she stood with her hands on her hips, staring at them and the twins as if this were her home and they were the trespassers.

"You the Kimball kids?" Her voice was shrill and high, and she did not even glance toward Libby. Nor did she wait for Christie to answer. "Tough luck, having to move again—"

What did she mean, move again? Perhaps the stranger read the bewilderment in Christie's expression, or else she was full of news she just had to tell.

"Your Dad made a bad bargain. This station's part of the G.T. spread now."

Christie was so startled she must have hugged Shan too tightly, for he gave a loud hiss and flattened his ears. What did the girl mean? She must be crazy—the station was their own! Father had said so and he had meant it. She caught her breath again and now determined that the girl was not going to frighten her with such a big lie.

Ignoring the stranger, she spoke to Libby. "Come on in, I'll get some towels and we can dry off." With her shoulders straight back, and her head firmly up, she marched by the Toner girl, her lips pressed tightly together.

7
Danger for Lady Maude

Just as it had been so noisy yesterday morning at the station, now it was very quiet. The workmen had left. Father had driven into town as soon as Mother had come back the day before to see someone at the bank. He was away a very long time. When Christie had gone to bed he had not yet returned, though when she awoke early in the morning the car was again standing in the untidy yard among the supplies to restore the station.

Was what Marlene Toner had said true? Did Mr. Toner really own the station and would the Kimballs have to move? Where were they going to go—back east again?

"Chris," Perks pattered over barefooted, her rumpled pajamas twisted about her legs, Raggedy Ann under her arm. Shan sat in the door of their room yawning, and Baron was outside barking, announcing it was time to feed a hungry dog.

"Chris," Perks repeated, tugging now at her sister's sleeve. "do we have to move?"

"I don't know. Anyway—not today."

"I don't want to go. Parky and Neal—they're going to open the treasure box. Chris, if there's money inside that—can't we give it to Daddy and help him keep the station?"

All the money in the world, Christie thought, might not make Mr. Toner let go of land he wanted. She knew that Father had been greatly worried yesterday—nearly as worried as he had been when he lost that job back in Mayfield.

"I know one thing," she said suddenly, "Marlene isn't going to get lady Maude!"

"But—how could she?" Perks wanted to know. "We found her—Marlene didn't."

"But if it's true her father owns the land where the cave is, maybe he can claim anything we found there belongs to him."

"We can hide her! Then if we have to go away we can take her along and that old Marlene won't even know about her."

That was an idea that had already occurred to Christie. She nodded. "We'll try that, Perks, if we have to."

It seemed that this was a day of troubles. First both Mother and Father had to go back into town. The children were given orders to stay with the Wildhorses. In fact, Mother and Father were in such a hurry to leave they said very little, except about what must be done and that Christie and Neal should take care of the twins and do what Mrs. Wildhorse told them.

Even Pinto was going with them. Perhaps, Neal and Christie decided, because he had lived at the station so long he knew more than anyone about who it really belonged to. He did not look like himself wearing a white shirt and a checked coat, with his hat on straight instead of pushed to the back of his head. And he was not happy-eyed anymore.

"We can clean up some." Christie tried to think of what might be done to help out as the car pulled away.

"You can," Neal told her shortly, "if you want to. I'm going to hunt in Pinto's place for a big hammer and a chisel. With those we can open the strongbox. If there's gold in that, Dad can sure use it now."

"But it wouldn't be our gold," Christie reminded him. "And besides, they said for us to stay right around here. We can't go to the cave today."

Neal hesitated. Their parents had been firm about that.

"We can go over to Toliver's. We can ask Mrs. Wildhorse. If she says it's all right, we can go."

"That—maybe that's being sneaky," Christie retorted. "You heard Mother say stay here."

"I'm not a sneak! You take that back!" Neal flared, his face flushing, his hand balling into fists. "I want to help Dad—and you say it's sneaky."

"Well, maybe not exactly sneaky. But you know Mother wouldn't want us to go as far as the cave."

Neal kicked a scrap of wood, sending it flying against the corral poles. Pinto had taken even the burros out to graze before he had left. The station seemed very lonely just now.

"I don't know what good it's going to do for us just to sit around here all day!" he burst out. "We could be opening that box, seeing what's in it."

Christie wavered. Maybe if Mother had known how important it was, she might have said they could go. But she had not and they *were* now bound by their promises.

Neal realized that, too. He kicked at another stick and then walked slowly toward the house. "All right, so we clean up," he said in a discouraged voice.

Christie looked sharply at the twins. "You two are to stay right here with Baron and Shan, remember?"

Perks nodded. Parky was squatting on his heels watching something on the ground with such absorption that he did not appear to hear.

"Parky!" Christie moved to stand over him.

"Yeah, I heard you." But he did not look up and Christie had to be content with that much of an answer.

Neal cleared off the table and stacked mugs and plates ready to wash while Christie went to make up the bunks.

"The stove fire's out," Neal called. "But some of the water still in the kettle ought to be warm yet. I just won't put any cold in with it."

She heard a lot of splashing, which meant Neal was washing up. But Christie's mind was busy with other thoughts.

Lady Maude must be worth a lot of money, and if they weren't going to be able to keep the station, then the plan of the museum would not work. Father must have spent a lot here buying things to turn the station into a motel. Mr. Toner might not pay for that because, as Toliver and Libby had said, he only wanted the water. If they could sell Lady Maude, maybe the money would help out a lot, bring enough to take them home again. Only—she felt a kind of pain even thinking of selling the doll.

Where could you sell her? To a museum, Christie supposed, or to some lady who collected old dolls. But how did you discover which museum or collector would want her? Did you advertise in a paper? Christie moved more and more slowly between each fold of blanket and smoothing of pillow.

"Hey, Chris, I'm finished washing—you come and wipe!" Neal called. "I'll sweep up while you do."

Hurriedly, Christie tidied the last bunk and came back to find Neal vigorously using the broom. He was just moving dust around instead of out, she told him indignantly as she reached for a dish towel.

"Just giving it a lick and a promise—that's what Pinto says when he sweeps," Neal announced. "Hurry up—we'll get the twins and go over to Toliver's. No use sticking around here." But he did come back to put the clean mugs back on the shelf while Christie carried the pan of dishwater to the door and poured it over the small bush Pinto had said was used to such refreshment.

It was when she looked around that she was aware of the unusual quiet. The twins— There was a sharp cry and she saw Shan tugging to reach to her. His leash had been made fast to a stone. But Baron and the twins were gone.

"Perks! Parky!"

As there was no answer to her urgent call, Neal came out.

"Neal—the twins—Baron—they're gone!"

"They probably ran on over to Toliver's. They knew we were going there."

"They weren't to go alone, Neal. We should have made them wait inside where we could watch them!"

"Oh, it's only a little way and Baron's with them."

"But there're snakes—and things." Christie felt shivery inside. She ran to Shan and gathered him up. "We've got to hurry and make sure they are there."

"Come on." Neal was already running down the trail toward the meadow. Surely the twins would have gone that way and not wandered off, thought Christie as she stumbled along.

She had hoped to overtake the children, or at least hear Baron's barks. But that did not happen. Libby sat on the step of the truck, a big bowl on her knees. She was stirring a mixture in it.

"Hi, Christie—" Then, seeing the expression on the other girl's face, Libby quickly put down the bowl and came to meet her. "What's the matter?"

"The twins—they've gone! Did they come here?"

Libby was already shaking her head. "I just came out. Mother told me to wait for you and bring you along. She's gone to paint and she took a picnic up canyon for us. Toliver went with her."

"But the twins!" Christie looked around wildly. They must have wandered into the bush. Baron—could Baron help? Neal already had his fingers to his lips and gave the carrying whistle that the big dog always answered.

115

"They may have gone to the cave," Libby suggested.

"Let's see!" Neal started on at a run.

"May I leave Shan here?" Christie detached Shan's claws from the tight hold on her shirt.

"Put him inside the van." Libby took up her bowl. When it and the protesting Shan were shut in, the girls pounded after Neal, who was almost out of sight.

As they reached the far end of the meadow Christie was startled by the nicker of a horse. Tied by reins looped over a bush was a golden mare with a creamy mane and tail. She was switching her tail back and forth impatiently.

"That's Spun Sugar, Marlene's horse," Libby said.

A short way beyond, the stamping, tail-switching Spun Sugar was at the entrance to the cave. A tumble of stones spilled out from the neat pile the boys had left. The girls could hear raised voices.

"Neal—Parky—" Christie recognized two of those voices as she pushed between the rocks to the cave entrance.

"Don't you dare touch that!" A shrill voice screamed. "Everything in here belongs to my father. You take anything and he'll have you arrested for stealing! You'd better get away from here fast."

"It's ours! We found it!" Perks now wailed loudly.

"Ouch! You nasty little boy! Bite *me*, will you?" There came a sound that could only be a slap followed by an outraged cry not of pain but of temper.

Parky! He used to bite—but that was only when he was little. Christie scrambled on into the cave, sending rocks tumbling. One of the camp lights was on and in its glow she saw that Lady Maude's box was open and the Lady herself partly unwrapped so she could be clearly seen.

Neal was holding Parky in spite of the little boy's struggles, his flying fists beating the air. Perks stood before Marlene, hitting out at the older girl as wildly as her brother fought to do.

"Perks!" Christie rushed to grab her sister. "Perks, behave yourself!" But she had difficulty restraining the child, who was red-faced now and screaming in rage.

"She slapped Parky, she did, she did!" The uproar Perks made was deafening.

"He bit me first!" Marlene had backed against the wall, staring at both furiously angry twins as if they were wild animals.

"She was going to take Lady Maude. She wouldn't let go of the box!" Perks continued. "She's mean, mean, mean!"

"Perks!" Christie shook her little sister. "Calm down, Perks. Stop it!" Now her voice was beginning to sound as shrill as Perks's.

"Get them out of here." Neal pushed the

resisting Parky ahead of him. Christie tried to follow his suggestion with Perks, though it was all she could do to force the little girl to take one step at a time. Meanwhile she heard a loud barking, as if Baron, having gone off on some business of his own, had returned to find his family in trouble and was voicing a warning about what he was going to do to remedy that.

Somehow they got the twins outside. Once in the open, they began to calm down. Parky refused to answer any questions and Perks cried loudly as Christie tried to find out what had happened.

"I'll tell you what happened," Marlene exclaimed. She had a tear in the sleeve of her shirt, and there were dark smudges on her jeans. "I saw these—these little monsters sneaking around, pulling out rocks to open up that cave. So I watched to see what else they were doing. That way I found this treasure of yours. They had just opened the box and were taking out that old doll when I caught them."

"Perks!" Christie's real horror was plain in her voice. What if the twins had dragged Lady Maude out, broken her fine china head, or gotten her dress torn and dirty?

"We were going to hide her and keep her safe!" Perks wailed. "You and Libby, you said she was worth a lot of money and we wanted her for Daddy! Then she"—Perks stabbed a finger toward Marlene—"said Lady Maude belonged to her and she was going to take her right now. When she couldn't let go of the box, Parky bit her. He had to—she wouldn't let go!''

''Just like an animal!'' Marlene broke in. ''Don't you teach your little brother to act human? Just like a dirty little animal—''

Christie gave Perks a push in Libby's direction and confronted Marlene. ''You—you shut up! Parky's no animal. He was just too excited and frightened. And you've no right to Lady Maude either!''

''So? Well, this cave is on my own father's land, and what's found here belongs to us! And—''

Marlene moved as if to return to the cave, but the four Kimballs plus Libby formed a solid barrier between her and its entrance. She stopped, but it was plain she was not yet defeated.

''You just wait and see! I'm going right home now and tell my father, and you'll see what happens to you then! Your little brother bit me and tore my shirt. See? Right here. You're keeping things that belong to us. My father, he'll fix you! Just wait and see!'' She turned her back on them and went toward her mare.

Neal moved as if to stop her, but Libby caught him back.

''Don't make it any worse,'' the Navajo girl advised him. ''She can cause trouble and she

will. What are we going to do about that now?"
She nodded at the cave.

"There's just too much for us to take it all
away," Neal said.

"Take the mail sack, Lady Maude, and the
strongbox," Christie advised. "The rest is
mostly old clothes. We can show Mother and
Father and they'll know who it really belongs
to."

"Chris—Chris, can Marlene do something
bad to Parky 'cause he bit her?" Perks caught
her sister's hand in both of hers and squeezed
it tight.

"Parky shouldn't have bitten—he knows
that," Neal said.

"Don't care!" Parky scowled at his brother
defiantly. "She was going to take our stuff.
She's nothing but an old stealer, so she is! I
couldn't make her let go, so I bit her!"

"You know what Daddy said about biting,"
Christie reminded him. "Now, we don't know
how long it will be before she comes back—"

"Yes." Neal turned to the cave. "We'd better get those things to the station as quick as
we can."

The mailbag was light enough for Perks and
Parky to carry between them. But Lady Maude's
box needed both Christie's and Libby's full
strength to transport it. Neal, with frequent
pauses to rest cramped fingers, carried the
strongbox. The meadow seemed to have dou-

bled in length when they crossed it so burdened.

"Yoooohooo!" Toliver ran to meet them from the van. "What's the matter? Why are you bringing that stuff here?"

Neal and Libby between them told him what had happened at the cave, while Perks and Parky dropped down beside Christie where she sat in the grass, one arm laid protectingly over Lady Maude's box.

"Christie, can—can she put me in jail?" Parky's face was not red with anger anymore. He did not look at his sister but stared at the ground. Perks squeezed up against him, putting an arm around his shoulders.

"No, I don't think so. But you shouldn't have done it—you know that."

"There was no other way I could stop her— she pulled so hard," he said miserably, and smeared one hand across his eyes.

"What made you go to the cave in the first place? If Marlene hadn't seen you there she wouldn't have known anything about it!"

"We wanted to get Lady Maude—for Daddy," Parky said.

"I'm going for Mother." Toliver broke away from Neal and his sister. "If old G.T. comes riding in here he won't listen to any bunch of kids. And Dad's gone off prospecting with Grey Eagle." The Navajo boy started to run and

Libby went into the van, coming out with a thermos jug and two paper cups.

"Here, Parky, Perks, drink some of this lemonade. You're all hot—it'll make you feel better."

Perks had cried so much she had hiccups and Parky's face was streaked with dust and tears. They drank what she had poured for them slowly. Christie stood up and drew a little away to whisper to Libby.

"Can Marlene really make a lot of trouble? About the bite and the things from the cave?"

"She can try." Libby did not give her any comfort. "Let's get these boxes and the mailbag into the van. Toliver will tell Mother all about it on the way back and she'll know better what to do. It'll take Marlene some time to ride home, and maybe her father won't be there. We can hope they won't come here until your folks are back, too. I wish Dad were here, but he won't be back until late tomorrow."

Christie shivered. It sounded as if they were in real trouble. Mostly it was her fault. If she had watched the twins more carefully, as Mother had expected her to, they would never have gone to the cave. Then Marlene would never have known about it. Parky was only a little boy. Surely they could not do anything to him really. But she was not sure of that.

She was still feeling cold inside when Mrs. Wildhorse came back with Toliver. The Navajo woman did not seem upset—only surprised at their finds. She agreed that they should leave those in the van for safekeeping—all except the mailbag.

"That should be delivered to the post office."

"They're dead letters." Parky had regained some of his usual assertiveness. "Neal said letters can't be delivered when they are dead."

"Perhaps they can't be delivered to the right people," Mrs. Wildhorse agreed, "but they are mail, in an official pouch, and must be taken to the office in town. I wonder how long they have been in that cave."

"The papers packed around Lady Maude have the date eighteen seventy-five on them," Christie said. "They were from London. Please, can Marlene just take Lady Maude and the rest of the things?"

"Not right away, and maybe not at all. We shall tell the sheriff about this and he will take charge. Perhaps even the court will have to decide about the true ownership. There's something even more important to think about now."

"You mean who's going to have the station?" Neal asked.

"Yes."

"Please, can you tell us more about that?" Christie wanted to know. "Mother and Father were so busy and they went to town so early.

All we really know is what Marlene told us—that her father and not Daddy owns it.''

"I don't think anyone knows the truth just yet, Christie. You see, when the stage line was established Arizona wasn't even a state—it was a territory. Mr. Bright, who started the stage line, had a grant from the territorial government to build the stations. But this particular one was built only with the permission of the Navajos by a special treaty.

"Then for a while it served also as an army post. So there have been a number of different 'owners.' The stagecoach rights were given to last a good many years, and they were renewed again right after Arizona became a state because no railway ran in this direction and there was another silver strike back in the mountains about fifty years ago. So, though the real stage had not run for a good many years, a transportation company was formed on their old charter and the station used again.

"Your father and his partner bought these rights from the representative of that old company. Now Mr. Toner says that because the stage line stopped using the station, they lost their claim and had no right to sell to a private person. It is all very complicated and may have to be taken to court.''

"That would take a long time, wouldn't it?'' Neal asked doubtfully.

"I'm afraid so.''

"And we can't wait a long time," Neal said. "We have to have the station open for business as soon as the highway is ready—Dad has said that several times. So it looks as if Mr. Toner may win after all."

"Why did the man sell it to Daddy if it didn't really belong to him?" Christie wanted to know.

"He thought that it did, and he will have to go to court, too," Mrs. Wildhorse said.

"But that still doesn't mean that Marlene can have Lady Maude and the rest of the things does it?" Perks leaned against Christie, again pulling at her hand. "It doesn't, does it?"

Christie could not answer that—she was too afraid that the answer might be yes, and inside now she felt as hot and angry as Parky must have been back in the cave. Nobody was going to get Lady Maude—not if she could help it!

8
Christie Writes a Letter

"You found all this hidden in a cave?" Father stared at the mailbag, Lady Maude's box, and the strongbox where they sat on the long table in the station house.

"There're some trunks and bags in there, too," Neal said. "But they've mostly just got clothes in them. And a shotgun—"

"But why would anyone wall up luggage and mail in a cave?" Mother questioned.

"Pinto told us a story about how once some men going east offered a lot of extra money to a driver to get them through when the Apaches were raiding. The driver knocked out the station man when he said they shouldn't go. They might have taken this extra weight out of the coach to go faster. But they were never heard of again," Neal continued.

"Why leave luggage in a cave instead of in the station itself?" Father wondered. "Well, no matter how it got there, you found it. And this"—he picked up the mail bag—"will certainly cause quite a stir. Its contents will be delivered quite a few years late."

"Dead letters." Parky relished those words. "Neal said they're dead letters."

"But Marlene can't have Lady Maude, can she?" Perks piped up. "She doesn't own her— or the treasure in there, either—" She pointed to the strongbox.

"It'll be for the court to decide." Father suddenly looked very tired. "Might as well get this into town tomorrow." He put the mailbag on top of the strongbox.

"Lady Maude, too?" Christie asked in a small voice. To have Lady Maude go out of her life so quickly was very hard.

Father hesitated. "Well, we can leave her and the other things you left in the cave until we find out what sort of claims can be made for those. But even if Toner gets the station, I don't see how he can claim any of this. We'll wait and see. This"—he patted the mailbag and the strongbox—"does have a place to go—the postal authorities."

"Is the strongbox like mail then?" Neal wanted to know.

"It probably took the place, in its day, of registered mail." Father looked around the room. "Nothing more we can do here now until we know more about things."

"If the people those letters were sent to are all dead now," Christie asked, an idea beginning to grow in her mind, "what will the post office do with them?"

"They may try to find descendants of those meant to have them," Father said. "Finding such mail will make exciting news. I remember reading some years back about a mail pouch that had been stolen over a hundred years ago and hidden under the floor of a house that was just being torn down. They tried to find the families of those the letters had been sent to—there was a story in the paper about it."

"Will they put a story in the paper about this, too?" Parky wanted to know.

"Could be. As for you, Patrick"—Father looked unsmilingly at Parky (to be called Patrick meant that Father was going to say something very serious)—"I think you had better go to your room and sit and think about what you did this morning. Do you remember what we said the last time this happened?"

Parky's face reddened. He looked down at the scuffed toes of his sandals.

"She—she wouldn't let go," he muttered.

"No excuses," Father answered. "March in there and think about it, Patrick. Also, decide what punishment meets this."

It *was* serious. Christie felt sorry for Parky

and glad she was not the one who had to leave the room. When Father was really upset he expected you to name your own punishment. You gave up something you wanted very much, generally because you were sorry enough to make it a stiff one. Or you did something you simply hated to do.

At least Mr. Toner had not arrived with the sheriff to arrest Parky. Christie had half-expected all afternoon to have that happen and had been so glad when Father and Mother got back from town. They had looked so unhappy and tired that she had made Neal and the twins wait until after supper to bring in the cave things.

"I think it's bedtime for all of you." Mother got up slowly, as if she were very tired indeed. She went to the sink pump and filled the big kettle and put that on to heat wash water. As she stood by the stove she looked slowly around the room, and Christie wondered if she were thinking about all the plans they had made. There had been the motor to run the refrigerator and a big freezer, a new stove, all the other things on the list that had been written out only a day or two earlier.

"Mother," Christie said later, when she was in her bunk and Mother had come in to tuck in Perks and say a last good night, "are we going to have to leave the station?"

"We don't know, Christie—we honestly

don't know." Mother sighed as she kissed Christie and went out. Shan purred loudly in Christie's ear and kneaded the pillow, up down, up down, with his dark brown paws, making a bed to his liking.

Mother did not know. Christie lay awake, watching the crack of light under the door. She could hear her parents still moving around, but they were not talking to each other. Then she heard their door shut.

Christie shivered. Perks must be asleep. In the quiet she could hear her sister's even breathing. Shan must be asleep too—he had stopped purring and his head was flat on the pillow where he stretched out limp and warm.

Now there were little noises Christie had not noticed before. A skitter-skatter sound on the roof overhead, and far off once an *ooo-ooo* which might have been a coyote and which Baron answered from the yard with a sharp bark.

When they had first come there Christie had been afraid of those noises. Back home, if you awoke in the night, what you could hear was the *woosh-woosh* of big trucks along the highway, or maybe once in a while one of the neighbors coming in late and closing a garage door with a bang.

Would the Kimballs now be going back to a house with a bathroom and water, a small yard, sidewalks all around? Christie found suddenly

that she did not want those things at all. She
wanted to stay right here. Oh, not as the station
was now, torn up and all untidy, but as it would
be when the workmen were through. She
wanted to be able to hunt arrowheads, and learn
to ride Sheba or Solomon, or perhaps even
someday a horse like Marlene's.

Marlene—and Lady Maude! Mother had
only just glanced at Lady Maude tonight—she
did not understand how wonderful she was. But
if Mother would really look at her and all she
had— And they had even told Mother and
Father about their plan. If they had to move,
there would be no plan—no one would ever
come to see Lady Maude and the other things
from the cave.

What they had said about postmen trying to
find the families of the people to whom the
"dead letters" had been written so long ago—
that stuck in Christie's mind now. What if
Maude Woodbridge had had a little girl of her
own, and in turn *she* had a little girl. Why, that
was who Lady Maude would really belong to!
And that would be better than Marlene getting
her.

Christie felt under her pillow for her flashlight, pressing the button, but keeping some of
her fingers over the bulb so only a little light
showed. There was just enough for her to be
able to find her suitcase. In that was the letter
Captain Woodbridge had written. Well, Chris-

tie could mail that. Only not give it to the post-men—no—she would send it in another enve-lope and she would write a letter to go with it, explaining all about the station and Lady Maude. Maybe there would still be some Woodbridge left to get it.

She did not know, of course, if there was any little girl now, or even if there was any such name or address—she could only use the one lettered on the box. However, if she put her own return address on the outside the letter would come back and then she could be sure there were no Woodbridges left.

Do it now—without telling anyone! She had the letter paper Grandmother Nourse had sent her—that with the Alice-in-Wonderland picture on it. Pinto could mail it for her—or Mrs. Wild-horse—she had said she was going to town to-morrow. Then, if there was no one to get the letter, Christie would be the only one to be disappointed. She must tell Pinto to send it fast mail—if the postman had that kind any more. For if Lady Maude were to be rescued, it must be soon.

Christie found her ballpoint and the writing paper. For a long moment she sat still on the lower bunk, listening. Yes, Perks was sleeping. She must be careful not to wake her. Using the paper box for a desk, she held the pen and tried to think carefully about what to write.

Should she say "Dear Maude Woodbridge"?

But it wouldn't be going to Maude now. What did you put at the beginning of a letter if you if you did not know just who was going to read it?

Perhaps that was just it. Since she did not know to whom she was writing, why not say so? With care Christie wrote at the top of the sheet: "Dear I do not know who—" It looked queer but it was the truth.

She had better explain right at the beginning. It took a long time to write the letter. First Christie had to tell who she herself was, then she had to describe finding Lady Maude and about the danger of losing her to Marlene. Twice she had to cross out words, and she was not quite sure about some of the spelling. Finally she had covered five sheets of paper. Now the envelope. For that there was only one possible address. Christie printed it so it would be extra plain.

"To the Family of Miss Maude Woodbridge, Woburnscott, Maine."

Her own address was in the upper corner and then *"urgent"* with two lines drawn under that.

When her five pages with the old letter were folded together, it made the envelope so fat Christie had to use Scotch tape to seal it shut. She tucked the letter and the flashlight under her pillow and settled down for the second time. Now she had only to ask Pinto to mail it. What if he wanted to know why? By this time Christie was so sleepy she could not stay awake to worry about that.

The next morning she had half-forgotten her letter. Mother had to call her twice, and Perks pulled the covers off her before she sat up blinking. But when she was dressing she remembered and hurried through shirt buttoning to get the fat envelope. It was so big and thick it might need two stamps—maybe even three. She still had some of her allowance left—enough, she was sure, to buy those.

All the family were already at the table when she came out. Father smiled at her.

"Not like you, Christie, to oversleep. You must have had a dream too good to lose," he said as she reached for a paper cup of orange juice.

"I can't remember any dream," she answered. "Is Pinto going into town today?"

"I was wondering," Father said, "how you and Neal and Perks would like to ride into town with us—to deliver the boxes and the bag to the post office and then tell the sheriff about them."

"Parky found them too," Perks said as she stirred her cereal around in her bowl.

"Parky has chosen to stay in his room today," Mother answered.

Perks stared mournfully into her bowl. If Parky had chosen that as his punishment, he thought it the worst that could happen to him

now. Perks looked as if she agreed with him—
to be separated from her twin was punishment
for her also. "I guess, then, I'll just stay here,"
she said in a low voice.

Father shook his head. "No, Perks. Parky
chose this and you must let him. You know the
rules. We shall go to town and next time Parky
will remember to think before he loses his temper."

Perks still looked unhappy as she and Christie went back into their room to put on clean
jeans and shirts. She stood staring at the floor
as Christie brushed her hair.

"Parky was just trying to keep Marlene from
taking Lady Maude. He wasn't being bad on
his own."

"He did it the wrong way, Perks. You know
that." Christie hunted for something to take
her sister's mind off Parky's troubles. "Listen,
Perks, you want to hear a secret?"

"What?" Perks asked flatly, still staring at
the floor as if nothing mattered very much.

"I've thought of a way to perhaps keep Lady
Maude from going to Marlene. Even if the sheriff says she can have her."

"How?" She did have Perks's attention now.

Christie showed her the fat envelope. "You
have to promise not to tell—not even Parky.
Because if anyone finds out too soon, maybe
it won't work." She hesitated. Telling Perks
was a risk.

"I always tell Parky everything," Perks said.

"Not at Christmas time," Christie reminded her. "Remember last year when you went along with Father to buy the talking bear? You knew for a long time that Parky was going to find that under the tree, but you never told."

"That was a Christmas secret."

"This is just as important a one. And it may help us out."

"How?"

Christie could not be sure. But anything that would keep Lady Maude from going to Marlene would help. "We'll just have to wait and see. You promise you won't tell, Perks."

"Cross my heart twice over?"

At Christie's nod the little girl thought for a long minute and then raised her hand to cross twice over. "I promise, Chris. Now—what's the secret?"

"You remember that letter we found in Lady Maude's box? Well, I put it in this envelope last night, and I wrote another letter to go with it, telling about how we found Lady Maude and what happened. I am going to mail this today when we go into town. We have to go to the post office anyway if Father takes the mailbag there."

"But who are you sending it to?"

Christie turned the envelope over so Perks could read the printing Christie had tried to make so plain. She had traced each letter twice to make sure.

"Remember what Father said about those letters going to families of the people who should have gotten them? I'm sending this to the family of Miss Maude Woodbridge, with the same address that is on the box. I put our return address on the outside. If no one gets it, then it will come back here and we'll know for sure that Lady Maude really belongs to no one."

"Then Marlene will get her?"

"Maybe not. We found her. Anyway, it can be a long time before anyone is certain."

"Chris." Perks watched her sister put the letter inside her shirt, count money out of her wallet and tie that into the corner of a handkerchief to be stuffed into her jeans pocket. "Are we really going to move again?"

"I don't know any more than you do, Perks. Listen—Mother's calling, we'd better go!"

Mother waved goodbye from the station doorway as Father turned the big car carefully to avoid all the things left by the workmen.

"What made you go looking for this treasure of yours?" Father asked as the car bumped and dipped on the rough road.

Neal told the story of Shan getting lost and how they had had to dig their way into the cave to find him.

139

"So we really have Shan to thank for it. Look, Perks, there goes a roadrunner!"

The long-legged bird raced along, almost keeping even with the car for a minute or two, then flashed off into the bushes.

"To think"—Father slowed down even more as they hit another very bumpy stretch—"this was considered a really good road at one time."

"Wonder what the stagecoach people would have thought of the big highway?" Neal asked.

"I am afraid they would not have had too comfortable a ride even on that in a stage-coach," Father said. "No springs—most of the coaches were slung on heavy leather straps. Lots of times on steep grades everyone had to get out and walk to spare the horses. Of course, on flat land they went as fast as anyone could in those days. I heard that the newspaper here in Gilesburg still stores the old station books. Nearest place Bright's heirs could find to keep them when the old line closed down. Perhaps we could get them back on loan, display them in this museum of yours."

Then Father's face changed and the eager look went out of it. He had just remembered, Christie knew, that perhaps they were not going to have the station after all. There would be no guests who would want to learn what life had been like in the old days.

"Isn't there a good chance of our staying,

Dad?" Neal must have read Father's expression as quickly as she did.

"It's a big tangle now. Bright had the franchise for the stage line under territorial law, before Arizona was a state. He also had the mail franchise from the U.S. government, which gave him certain privileges. People were not so careful about land rights and things of that sort back in the days when this was all wilderness and there was a lot of unclaimed land. Too, Bright had a slightly different case with our station than with the rest of his holdings. It is partly over the border of the Navajo reservation, so he had a treaty with them later. Also, the army once used it as an outpost. So there were a number of different regulations. Colby thought our title to the station was solid—it came directly from the liquidation of the stage company. We never expected any trouble, though Colby knew that Toner was after the water rights. He had already told Toner he would not sell.

"Now Toner thinks he can prove Colby never had any right here in the first place. We can't count on anything until it's legally decided. If we had a year, maybe two, with the new highway open and tourists coming through to the park, we could make it. Colby has an idea about opening a side trail up to that ghost town, Darringer. He's out in Hollywood right now trying to interest some show people in restoring part of the town as an attraction. It has been done in other places. We could link the station to that also as a part of the old stage history. That's why we planned to rebuild so it would look just as it did in the old days. I've wired Colby and he'll be back as soon as he can. If Toner is determined to fight this through the courts, we might not be able to afford to stand up to him. Legal help is very expensive—"

Father sounded more as if he were thinking aloud, speaking of all that was on his mind rather than talking to them. Christie sighed. Their own plan would have worked out so well with all Father had wanted to do.

Maybe Father heard her sigh, for he glanced down and smiled. "Trouble has a way of hanging around, but that's no reason to invite it to come and live with us. We don't have to move out yet. Colby may not only have some ideas about how to handle Toner, but he's going to be very excited about this find of yours. I don't think he's ever seen before the cargo—if you can call it that—of a stagecoach intact after a hundred years."

They went to the sheriff's office first when they came into town. It was not the least like a sheriff's office in the TV Westerns, Christie discovered, but more like a real office. One man was using a typewriter, and there was no big wall rack with guns in it or an old stove with a coffeepot sitting on top.

The man who met them did have on boots and a wide-brimmed hat hung on the rack by the door. He wore a gun belt with a holstered gun and a badge pinned to the breast pocket of his khaki shirt.

"I'm Wylie." He held out his hand to Father. "You're Kimball—heard about you from Lucas when he passed through. What can I do for you?"

"Well, maybe you can tell us just what to do with this." Father set the strongbox down on the nearest desk, the mail sack laid across it. "I suppose the mail goes on to the post office—about a hundred years late!"

The sheriff looked for a moment as if he was not quite sure he had actually heard what Father had said. Then he turned his head and stared at the pouch and the box, almost as if he expected them to explode. The man who had been typing swung around in his chair to stare, too.

"A hundred years," the sheriff repeated, as if to make sure that really was what Father had said. "Suppose you tell me just what we have here anyway!"

Father did just that—telling about the cave, the lost luggage, and all the rest of the story, while the sheriff looked more and more surprised.

"A strongbox—and mail—" he repeated when Father had finished. "This is something to make eyes open around here. A story like this"—he shook his head—"well, I guess you have the evidence, so the case is proven all right! But you've got yourselves a real mystery story, you sure have!"

9
Visitors

"Talk about instant publicity!" Mother leaned back in her chair and pushed a straying wisp of hair off her forehead. "Marina, just *look* at that crowd!"

"If the motel were only open for business now!" Marina Wildhorse smiled as she glanced through the nearest window at the many cars parked around the station yard.

There was the sheriff's with its big star on the door. Next to that one the post office man had come in. But those were only the first two. Behind was one from the newspaper, and then two owned by town council members. Crowding into what space was left were others, belonging to who knew who.

Christie counted. Ten, eleven, twelve! And another was raising a dust cloud on the road!

There would not be any parking space for that one unless he just pulled to the side of the road outside the station yard.

"And the local TV-radio station people—the blue car's theirs," Mother continued. "That man has been positively besieging us. Wants the children and everything they found to be featured on some program. It's beyond belief!"

At least now, Christie and Neal had decided privately between themselves when they had seen the excitement begun in the sheriff's office, growing greater as they went to the post office, Marlene would have to work to prove that *she* had any right to Lady Maude. Why, the postmaster had sent a telegram about their find to Washington, and when they had opened the strongbox they had discovered a small bag of gold dust and some important papers inside.

It was then that the newspaperman had come with a camera and followed them all the way back to the station, taking pictures—even of Shan, because Shan had really found the cave. Other men had asked them about a million questions. Christie was afraid Shan's picture was not going to be very good—he was spitting at his dislike of the whole affair when it had been taken. Though it was late afternoon now, still more people continued to come.

"You've been feeding them," Mrs. Wildhorse said.

"Yes. They've about cleaned us out of a

week's supplies. Look here—they left all this by their plates." She had a small bowl with money in it. "I don't know who left what. They kept coming and going, so I couldn't return it."

"Why should you? After all, you are or are going to be in business here. Just use that to replace your supplies."

"Who would ever think of something such as this happening?"

"Gilesburg is not a city, though it would like to think it is," Mrs. Wildhorse commented. "I think that the newspaper, the TV, the council members are all very much aware of the value of publicity. They want to promote tourism here. Most of them must think this is a wonderful way to begin. After all, this find is probably unique—what must have been the complete cargo of a stagecoach in excellent condition—to say nothing of the mystery of where and why it was left. Also, there is the added attraction of Lady Maude—who can resist her?"

She nodded to a small table at the other side of the room where the doll, carefully unwrapped, stood, her fantastic wardrobe spread out around her, just as she had been placed for a whole series of photographs.

"She alone ought to bring a big price, if you want to sell her."

"We don't know who has the right to sell her," Mother answered. "Not that that matters at present. What I am wondering is how this will affect Mr. Toner's claim."

"That will get a good talking over today. Every sightseer out here knows all about what he is trying to do. It's a good thing you don't have a phone connected yet. At least you don't have a lot of calls to plague you."

"Small mercies thankfully received." Mother laughed. "This is like being caught in a rush hour on the subway, with the role of short-order cook added. I'm holding back enough food for our own supper and looking forward to when I can say, 'We've no more supplies. Sorry.' Only I shan't be sorry really."

Christie was only half-listening—rather she was thinking about this morning in the post office. While Father and the sheriff, with Neal tagging behind, had gone in to see the postmaster in his private office, she had bought her stamps and had pushed her fat letter through the slit in the wall marked OUT OF TOWN. If there was anyone to get that letter it might be soon decided about Lady Maude.

"Howdy, ma'am." A tall young man stood just outside the door. "I have a telegram for Mr. Harvey Kimball. You know where I can find him?"

Mother shook her head. "Just now he might be anywhere. Up at the cave—or—well, just anywhere. I haven't seen him for about an hour. I'm Mrs. Kimball, can I take it?"

"This says Mr. Kimball." The young man looked doubtful. "But seein' as how you're his missus, I expect it's proper. Say, whatever is goin' on here anyways?"

"Do you mean"—Mrs. Wildhorse laughed—"there is one person left in Gilesburg who doesn't know about the treasure?"

"Treasure. You mean that one of them there lost mines has been found?" The young man glanced at the crowded yard. "How come the sheriff's mixed up in something like that?"

"Not a mine, no. They just found some things taken off one of the old stagecoaches and walled up in a cave."

"I'll be! Could that be off the ghost stage maybe?"

"The ghost stage?" Christie moved closer. "What's the ghost stage?"

The young man looked as if he were sorry he had mentioned the subject. "Oh, that's just a story the old-timers used to tell to scare little kids around here. They said that there was a stage pulled out of here in Indian times and was never seen again. The rest of the story is that some people have seen it running along the old road in the moonlight, not making any noise, but with the horses going full gallop. It's just one of them old stories, ma'am," he said to Mother, as if to reassure her.

"Interesting," she answered. "But hardly to be wished for. That road's pretty narrow. I'd hate to have to share it with a wild-running ghost stage at night.''

You won't, ma'am. Just an old story. Say, is it all right if I look around some?''

"No reason not to," Mother answered. "Just follow the trail beyond the corral."

"You see?" Mrs. Wildhorse came away from the window to take a humming kettle off the stove and pour steaming water into a dishpan. "There's another ready-made tourist attraction—a ghost stagecoach."

"I can do without any more attractions for the time being, and probably for quite a while! Listen, Marina—you mustn't try to wash all these. Just let me—"

"I shall wash and Christie will dry, while you rest. If you must do something, work out your grocery list. Make it large—you may have visitors for more than just today. Even if Jim Wylie carts everything back to town, there'll be people out to see where it was found."

Mrs. Wildhorse began to wash mugs and plates, while Christie dried and piled them in the old wall cupboard. They were still using as many paper plates and napkins as they could, but most of those were gone now. Mother got a tablet and a pencil and started a list.

"Give it to Jim when you're finished," Mrs. Wildhorse said. "He'll drop it off at the market. They'll truck it out."

"This far? They wouldn't!"

"Sam Birke drives the truck and it's a wonder he isn't out here now. Sam wants to be a history teacher. He'll be very glad of a good excuse to learn what's going on. No—save yourself all you can—do it that way."

"Mother"—Libby ran in—"one of those men from the TV car, he went over and looked in the van windows—then he wanted to know if you were *that* Marina and were you painting some more pictures now? I slipped out through the bushes. Toliver's taken the horses and the burros and gone up canyon with Pinto. The newspaper people took Pinto's picture twice, and he said if they tried it again he'd fix them good. He's so mad he won't talk to anyone now."

"Oh, dear!" Mother gave a big sigh and laid down her pencil. "Everyone is going to be upset before this is over. How the children can sleep through this racket." She got up and went to look into the room into which the twins had retired earlier. "It's so hot, and I've started a headache."

"Now it's your turn to go and lie down. Take an aspirin and do it right now! Christie, Libby, and I can manage beautifully. You Kimballs have had more than your share of troubles these past two days."

Mother tried to protest, but Mrs. Wildhorse hurried her off. Christie went to look in on the twins. Baron lay on the floor by one bunk, where Parky was stretched out, staring straight up. Perks was actually asleep, curled in a knot on her own bunk with Shan on the pillow beside her.

"What do you want?" Parky demanded in a hoarse whisper as Christie tiptoed over.

"Mother thought you were asleep."

"I'm being punished." His whisper came a little louder. "That's why I'm here. And if you come and talk to me, it isn't being punished. So you just keep away—hear?" He put his fingers in his ears and squeezed his eyes tightly shut.

Christie obediently slipped away. Poor Parky—he had chosen a very hard punishment. It did not mean just staying in his room and not going into town, but had also turned out to be missing all the exciting things that had happened since. However, Mother had said he was to come out and have his picture taken with the rest of the children. After that Parky had marched right back to his self-imposed imprisonment, where Perks had joined him in the early afternoon.

Libby and her mother were in front of the table where Lady Maude stood. Christie sighed as she joined them. There was very little chance, she was sure, of keeping the doll. It would be such fun to try on all those clothes—to dress her in the lovely brocade ball gown with the long kid gloves or see her in the pale green dress Mother said was called a morning gown or the tea dress of pink satin trimmed with red velvet for a front panel.

"Even a card case!" Mrs. Wildhorse had picked up a tiny mother-of-pearl case and opened it to show wee cards packed inside. "Everything! I don't think there has ever been so completely equipped a fashion doll seen before in this day and age. She is truly a museum piece."

"Just so, dear lady."

They turned, startled. There was a man in the doorway. He was short and his coat was off, hanging over one arm, while with his other hand he mopped his round red face. His thin, turtle-necked shirt had damp spots on the shoulders, and big black sunglasses hid his eyes.

"Simmons, I'm Arthur Simmons, ma'am." He gave a little nod of his head. "Probably never heard of me, but I've been hearing a lot about you—and this find. Just pure luck my passing through when the news broke. I'm an NBC man—"

"You mean the TV network?"

"That's right. Local man told me about this—" He glanced around the big room. "Heard you were restoring a stage station. Quite famous once, wasn't it? So this is the doll—" He marched up to Lady Maude's table, still wiping his face, now and then running the handkerchief over the top of his bald head for good measure. "Now will you look at that! Pretty near everything a lady of her day would need. Who was she being sent to—do you know?"

"Miss Maude Woodbridge of Woburnscott, Maine," Christie told him.

"Poor Miss Woodbridge," Mr. Simmons said. He sounded, Christie thought, a little surprised, as if he were really sorry that Lady Maude had never reached her destination. "But I wonder how and why this lady was in Hong Kong. Too bad she can't tell us, isn't it? However, she's a natural, she certainly is—along with all the rest. I'll call Stan tonight—"

"A natural for what, Mr. Simmons?" Mrs. Wildhorse wanted to know.

"For our See America program, Mrs. Kimball. Strange and unusual bits of American lore brought to the screen—"

"I'm not Mrs. Kimball. And I think you had better get the Kimballs' permission before you plan anything. Mrs. Kimball is not feeling too well and is resting. Mr. Kimball may be up at the cave with some of the local authorities—"

"Certainly we'd clear everything with the Kimballs, Mrs.—Mrs.—"

"Wildhorse."

Christie saw Mr. Simmons give a little start. "Mrs. Wildhorse—but then you're Marina, aren't you? I thought I recognized this little girl," he nodded at Libby. "This *is* my lucky day! That is, if you, ma'am, are willing to co-operate, too. Your paintings have aroused a great deal of attention and you are one of the persons I came here to contact for the program."

"Another 'strange and unusual piece of American lore,' Mr. Simmons?"

"About the most American lore to be found nowadays," he returned. "But only with your complete cooperation, of course."

"I'll think about it. You look very hot, Mr. Simmons. Would you like a cool drink?"

"Now that is about the kindest suggestion I've had made to me in some time. If you could spare me a seat, too—"

Christie went to get some of the lemonade they made with the cold spring water. When she came back Mr. Simmons was sitting on one of the hard-bottomed chairs, looking around intently. He had taken off his sunglasses and was surveying the walls of the room one by one, as if he wanted to remember just where every nail was placed in them.

"This is certainly going to be a natural—"

His murmur was interrupted by a pounding at the screen door. Christie, who was nearest, opened it and found herself facing a very tall, thin man with a narrow face that had deep lines about the mouth and nose. He looked at her sharply.

"You one of the Kimball kids?"

"I'm Christie Kimball." Then she knew who he was, though she had seen him only once when he was getting into his station wagon. "You're Mr. Toner."

"I'm Toner. What in thunderation is going on here anyway? Had to park way back on the road—" He broke off his own sentence to demand harshly, "Where's your dad, kid? I've got a paper for him, a very important paper."

"He may be up at the cave with Sheriff Wylie."

"So Jim Wylie's here? Well, that's all the better. He can see what your dad will have to do. That the doll Marlene's been talking about?" He shoved past Christie to examine Lady Maude and her belongings. "Looks old—must be worth somethng. You can pack her up—I'll just take her and the rest of her gear along with me—"

"I don't think so." Mrs. Wildhorse moved in to stand between Lady Maude and Mr. Toner. "Sheriff Wylie has temporary custody of all the things discovered in the cave. The Kimballs officially turned them over to him this morning."

"Found on my land, weren't they? I'll settle it with Jim—"

"Before you touch anything," answered Mrs. Wildhorse, "you will check with the sheriff. You will find him and Mr. Kimball at the cave if you wish to discuss this matter with them.''

''Don't need any discussion. Matter of law—Kimball's out, I'm in. Wylie's going to explain it to him if he doesn't understand it already. I'll be back for the doll. Marlene's taken a fancy to it. Kimball ought to be glad I'm not suing him for what his kid did to my girl. He's getting off easy!''

Mr. Toner swung around and stamped out, slamming the screen door behind him.

''Pleasant gentleman, that.'' Mr. Simmons broke the following silence. ''Do you mind telling me what that was all about? Just curiosity on my part, of course. If it's too personal, you needn't answer.''

''Mr. Toner has been trying to get title to this land for some time,'' Mrs. Wildhorse explained. ''The water rights are quite valuable. Now it turns out there may have been some flaw in the title when the Kimballs took it over. The case is very complicated, since it involves both the old state franchise and an Indian treaty. His daughter followed the children to the cave and saw the doll. Since then Mr. Toner's effort to take possession have speeded up.''

''He doesn't sound like a very good neighbor—''

Mrs. Wildhorse made no comment. ''He

wants the land badly. A never-failing spring in this country is rare."

"Interesting. Thanks for the drink. I guess I'll go up and have a look at the cave, too." Mr. Simmons put on his sunglasses and his coat and left. Christie was hardly aware he had gone. She was too busy thinking about what Mr. Toner had said. Could he just take Lady Maude and make them move right now, as he threatened?

Slowly she turned once more to stare at the doll. It was almost as if Lady Maude were unlucky—they had had nothing but trouble ever since they found her. Christie began to wish she had never seen her at all.

"Shall we pack up her things?" she asked Libby's mother. "Maybe the sheriff will say that Mr. Toner can take her—"

"I think it would be well to pack her away now that the pictures have been taken," Mrs. Wildhorse agreed. "But I do not believe Mr. Toner will take her—not today, and perhaps never. If they cannot find anyone who owns her now, she might even belong to the state of Arizona. Which means she will be put in a museum, where everyone can enjoy seeing her."

Christie and Libby went to wash their hands. Then, with the greatest of care, they began returning all the wardrobe to the proper trunks and boxes. Each of those in turn was settled into the metal box in proper order. Lady

Maude, once more thoroughly wrapped, was put in last. Mrs. Wildhorse examined the address painted on the lid.

"Miss Maude Woodbridge, Woburnscott, Maine. But, Christie, how did you know that she was sent from Hong Kong—there is nothing here to say that?"

"There was a letter about her—inside," Libby answered first, and Christie was sorry she had not warned the Navajo girl not to mention that. "It said that her father could not get home for her birthday and he was sending Lady Maude east with the mate from his ship."

"Where is the letter now?"

Both of them looked to Christie. She would have to tell—no keeping her secret now. Anyway, perhaps the letter would come back.

"I—I mailed it—to the address. Dad said they would try to find the families of the people to whom the letters in the bag were written. So I wrote a letter, too, and put it with the letter from the box. I sent it to the family of Miss Maude Woodbridge in Maine. I did not want Marlene to have her—not if there was maybe a Woodbridge girl who could claim her. She *would* belong to her, wouldn't she?" Christie appealed to Mrs. Wildhorse.

"I would certainly think so, with the old letter to prove it. But, Christie, it would have been better to let the post office officials trace the letter."

"Marlene said she was going to take her. Maybe she could if it took a long time to trace people." Christie felt very uncomfortable. Probably Mrs. Wildhorse was right, but somehow she was still glad that she had sent that letter.

"Well, it's done now—and perhaps you will be lucky." Mrs. Wildhorse went to the cupboard and started checking over the few supplies still there. "Suppose you help me now to finish making out your mother's grocery list. If you will write down what I tell you—"

Christie was relieved nothing more was said about her letter. She gladly took up the tablet and the pencil. "Mother has some things here already—sugar, beans, bacon, peanut butter, jam, bread—"

"Coffee," Mrs. Wildhorse dictated, "canned peaches, some mixes—say, gingerbread, and biscuits, and a couple of cake ones—matches, syrup, pancake mix, onions, potatoes—"

"That sounds like an awful lot," Libby commented.

"Judging by today, they are going to need every bit of it," her mother answered. "Put down lemonade mix, Christie, crackers, cheese, cookies—I would say that visitors here are only beginning to come. Even more will come over the weekend."

Christie hoped they would not. She did not mind people like Mr. Simmons and some of the others. But Mr. Toner—if he could be counted as visitor—she did not want to see him again!

Mr. Toner was like a big black shadow stretching over the whole station, tall and thin though he was. She did not want to think about him and what he said. But she kept doing so in spite of all her efforts.

10
Ghost Town

"This is just a lull before another storm, I suppose," Father said. "At least no one has shown up yet this morning. Maybe they'll hold off if Wylie sets things in motion at the courthouse. I'll be glad of a breathing spell. One good thing—the publicity has tied Toner's hands for a while. Wylie and the council members informed him that his court order is suspended in the public interest. Wylie told me he's making a point of seeing Judge Framely to that effect this morning. He was very sure Framely would agree."

"All this uncertainty." Mother shook her head. "We're worse than just camping out now. I never know when I'll have to be packing up again. And that mess out in the yard—"

"I know. When Colby gets here we surely

must be able to sort everything out. He said over the phone he's making it in at least two days. Meanwhile, Patricia, we'll just have to sit tight and do a lot of hoping. However, we can turn to in the yard and clear up some of that. If the public descends upon us again in flocks—or droves—or whatever you want to term it—of cars, we can make slightly more room. If we didn't have this trouble with Toner, all this publicity would be the best thing we could hope for. Simmons wants to bring in his traveling TV crew as soon as they reach Gilesburg.''

There was no news from Sheriff Wylie, and, while a few cars did come out from town (the delivery truck from the market one of them), there was no jam-up in the yard such as there had been before. Christie was counting days impatiently. She could only guess how long it might take her letter to reach Maine—maybe a week. Then, if the postman did know a Woodbridge family, how long would it be before an answer came? Always assuming they would answer at all. To her even one week seemed to be a very long time.

However, they were not just going to sit around waiting for anything—Mr. Toner, a letter, or the sheriff. They helped Father pile and store into neater stacks the material to be used in restoring the station. Pinto came back out of hiding, though he still disappeared quickly into the smithy at the arrival of any new car, slamming the door behind him. Nor did he bring the horses and the burro family back into the corral, stating that visitors upset them.

"I'd say we've done a pretty good day's work," Father announced that evening. "In fact we've done so well we deserve a vacation. So suppose we each think of what we would like to do most. You first, Pat." He looked to Mother.

"Really want to do?" She laughed. "Really truly?" That was what Parky always asked.

"Really truly!" Father said firmly.

"Then I would like to go in to town, have my hair washed and set, get a facial, and have a dinner I haven't cooked myself in a nice air-conditioned restaurant."

She paused, looking from one to another of them. "I see my kind of really truly is not in favor with the rest of you. But suppose I say it is really truly for me alone, that none of the rest of you have to share it? Would that be all right? You see, Marina has an appointment with Mr. Simmons, who wants to interview her on TV. I could ride in with her, so I wouldn't need the car."

"Done!" Father slapped his hand down on the table so hard his coffee mug bounced. "Now—Perks, Parky. What's your really truly." The twins always chose the same thing, so a single question was all that was needed.

"Go out there." Parky waved a hand toward the open door. "See some place we haven't been to before."

"Christie?"

She was undecided. It would be nice to go in town with Mother. But just sitting around waiting at the beauty shop would be boring.

"I don't know—maybe to go off, like Parky said."

"Neal?"

He was excited and ready. "I'd like to go and see the ghost town Pinto told us about—Darringer. I've never seen a ghost town—except on TV."

"And you, Harvey?" Mother asked the question now.

"Oddly enough, I had Neal's suggestion in mind. Lucas is back and would be willing to guide us. Libby and Toliver would probably like to go along—leave you girls free for your day in town. As I understand, there's enough of a road left so we can use the station wagon. I want to take some pictures. We can carry a picnic lunch and water with us."

"You think it wise—just to leave here, I mean?" Mother asked.

"Now that all the 'treasure' is safe in town, yes. Nothing worth taking here. If any sightseers come, they can poke around and Pinto will keep an eye on things. Be a good idea for all of us to get away for a day. However, if we're going to Darringer we'll have to get an early start. That means bedtime for all you adventurers now."

"What do adventurers do?" Perks wanted to know.

"Have adventures—like explorers," Neal answered. "We were adventurers when we found that cave, weren't we, Dad?"

"Very much so, I would say."

"Maybe we'll find something at Darringer!" Parky was excited.

"Don't get your hopes up too high, Parky. Darringer has been visited by a lot of explorers. I'm afraid you can't count on much luck there. Now bed for each and every one of you—and that pronto!"

"Chris," Perks said as they settled down for the night, "does a ghost town have real ghosts in it?"

"Of course not! It's just a town where everybody moved off and left the buildings standing empty. You know—like on the TV when a cowboy rides into one of those places and there are tumbleweeds blowing around and he's all alone—"

"But sometimes there're bad men hiding out there waiting to get him," Perks said uncertainly.

"That just happens in stories, Perks. Father and Mr. Wildhorse will be with us. No, this is just an empty town we're going to—nobody's lived there for a long time."

"Why did everyone go off and leave it?"

"Because there wasn't any more silver to be dug out of the mines there. Most of the men worked in the mines. So when there was no more work they had to go and find someplace where there was."

"Oh." Perks seemed satisfied.

Christie lay in her bunk with Shan purring into her ear and thought about Darringer and the ghost towns she had seen on TV. Perks was right about the hero always getting into trouble in one. Usually someone was hiding out, ready to start a fight. But that was only in stories. All they would see would be some lizards and spiders in the old buildings.

It was early the next morning when they were called. And on the table in the big room there was not just one picnic basket but two. Father filled the canteens and some extra water bottles and Mother put out breakfast.

"There's supposed to be a spring near the town, but the old pumps are certainly not working," Father said. "Water is the one thing we want to be sure we have. Lucas will load some, too." He screwed the lid on the last container. "I suppose Shan is going as well as Baron?" He looked to where the brown cat was crunching dried food from his bowl.

"We couldn't leave him!" Christie was startled. "Even if we shut him in here, someone might open the door and—"

"Then be sure he has his leash on, and you'll be responsible for him, Christie."

"Yes, Father," she answered through a mouthful of cereal.

Before they were through breakfast the Wildhorse family had arrived. Lucas and Father loaded the cans of water and the baskets into the back of the station wagon, along with some bundles the Navajos had brought. Baron jumped into his usual place behind. The children took the middle seats while Lucas and Father were in front. They waved goodbye to Mother and Mrs. Wildhorse and were on their way.

For a while they followed the town road. Then, at Lucas's direction, Father swung off to the north. Now and then there were faint traces to be seen on the ground as if this too had once been a road. But the riding was even more bumpy than on the town road and Father drove very slowly.

"The new highway cuts northwest within about two miles," Lucas was saying. "To open a trail in from that direction would be the best. You might get some backing from Gilesburg for that. After all, the town wants all the tourist trade it can get. Darringer would make a good added attraction to people going to and from the park. Does your partner intend trying any restoration?"

"Depends on what interest he can raise in such a project. A lot of Hollywood money is going into such schemes now—Disney paved the way. There certainly isn't much road left here—that's sure. Can we make it by car?"

"You could last year. Movie outfit came here looking for an authentic background. They were here for about a week, then there was a flash flood and they cleared out. My cousin Brad set up their camps for them. Now—wait a minute!" Lucas pushed forward in the seat to survey the ground ahead. "Yes—see that rise over there? You turn here, use that for a guide point. Now—see those ruts—" He pointed to depressions in the ground. "Ore wagons made those. In spite of all the time gone by since then, those have been left to mark the road."

"When did the last digging close down?"

"Let's see. The Letty Bell was working about quarter time back in nineteen twenty. She ran out a couple of years later. There were still some small pockets where men held on maybe two, three years longer. The rich ore was gone and what was left cost too much to extract. I don't know when the last of the small operators closed. Been no one there since I can remember. Some of the prospectors use the town for a camp now and then while they poke around the hills, but no one else goes there."

"When did the first mine open?"

"Slim Gordon made the big strike there in eighteen seventy. He'd been nosing around before the Civil War and staked out then what he thought was a promising claim to come back to later. Even put up his monuments—"

"Monuments?"

"That's how they staked their claims in the old days. A man built a pile of stones and put a tin can inside, sealing in the can the description of the section he claimed. Sometimes it might be weeks before he could get in to register it legally. Well, Gordon did that in '60 on his first trip before the war broke out. Then he could not get back here until the army came in again. He found that claim was a rich one—the Western Star. Later he opened up the Good Chance, too. Sold out in eighteen-eighty and went to California. He was getting along in years and wanted to live soft for a while. But others had followed him. Now—angle right here—"

The station wagon bumped on. Sometimes they could still see the old ruts of the forgotten road, other times there were no marks at all. They came closer and closer to the hills and now more ruts showed plainly. The car climbed up a small hill, then a higher one. Father stopped there so all could see ahead into a dip between the hills, which grew taller the farther they stretched away.

There were buildings ahead. Some were of

wood, some of adobe. Most stood in two strag-
gling lines with what might have once been a
street between. More were scattered around on
the slopes of the hills. Some no longer had
roofs. In others part of a wall had fallen, letting
the roof sag at a corner.

"That's Darringer," Lucas told them.

Father drove the car very slowly down the
slope and into the main street, moving between
buildings where doors and windows had bits of
board nailed across them. Above the doors of
some where faded names, mostly so far gone
they could not be read at all.

"See that?" Lucas half-turned in his seat to
point out one building to the children. "That's
the end of the Bright Stage Line—the Darringer
office."

"Look, Dad, see? It says 'sheriff'!" Neal
pointed to the next building.

Baron barked and pushed his head between
Neal and Toliver. Even Shan put his forepaws
on the edge of the window to look out.

"Can we go and look inside, Daddy?" Parky
asked. "I want to see the sheriff's office!"

"Shades of Wyatt Earp," laughed Lucas.
Then he looked at them all, his face once more
sober. "We stick together. You don't go anyplace unless we say so, understand? The boards
in the floors are rotten, the walls and roofs
shaky—it could be dangerous."

"You mind what Lucas says." Father backed

him sternly. "This is no place to go exploring on one's own."

They had started very early, before the sun was up. Though it was much later now, there were still clouds overhead. Lucas studied those thoughtfully as they got out of the car.

"Rain coming. We'd better see if any building can give us shelter if it hits hard." He had a flashlight ready as they came to the rotted boardwalk that led to the doors of the old stage station and the sheriff's office.

The windows of both were boarded up by slats of wood crisscrossed over them. But their doors hung open. Lucas flashed his light into a dim interior and then walked forward cautiously. They could hear him stamping inside the stage office as if to make sure the floor was safe. Then he waved to them from the door.

"This is okay. Not much left, though."

They crowded in behind Father, Shan clinging to Christie's shoulder, Baron nosing around and then giving a big sneeze as if he had sniffed up a lot of dust. There was a counter across the room and shelves in the wall behind it. An old rolltop desk with its top stuck halfway down stood to one side. Next to that was an iron safe with gold lettering—Bright Stage Line. Dust and dead flies lay everywhere. Christie thought it looked miserable but Father had out his camera with flash bulbs and was taking pictures.

"How about the sheriff's office, Dad?" Neal

asked. "If it's all right to go in there, it ought to be more exciting than this—"

"Right—sheriff's office it is."

They detoured around the worst holes in the plank walk and for the second time Lucas went in first.

"Smells funny," Perks whispered to Christie, and Christie agreed, lingering by the door with Libby as the boys pushed in.

"Father, if we promise to stay with the car, can we stay outside?" Christie wanted to know. She did not like the darkness nor the smells at all. And there was nothing to see really but old broken furniture and floors with holes in them.

"Right by the car, yes." He was busy taking pictures again.

The two older girls, trailed by Perks, went out. Christie breathed the fresh air thankfully and looked around with more interest at the town itself. There was no sun breaking through the clouds and it felt chilly. She was glad they had brought sweaters.

"I wonder if any girls like us ever lived here?" She looked down the street and the lines of falling-to-pieces buildings and tried to imagine what Darringer had been long ago—that was easier to do than when one looked at all the broken rooms inside.

"There must have been some children,"

Libby said. "Maybe there's a school somewhere. See that steeple—that was a church."

The steeple was crooked—another wind-
storm might well send it crashing to the ground.
Shan kicked to get down and Christie let him
jump into the thick dust of the street, but kept
careful hold on his leash. He smelled the ground
and then sneezed as Baron had done. Nor did
he pull at the leash as if he wanted to go off on
his own.

They could hear voices from the sheriff's
office, but the rest of the town was very quiet.
Suddenly a crash startled them all.

"Christie!" Father shouted.

"We're here!"

He ran out of the office looking anxious.
"That noise—"

"It came from there somewhere." She
pointed.

"Probably part of an old building falling.
See? That's why you must not go off on your
own."

That was the last thing Christie wanted to do.
The town was—spooky. It made her feel as if
people were hiding, peeking at her from between the slats nailed over the windows or from
behind the sagging doors. She could understand
very well why such places were called "ghost
towns." Perhaps they really were homes for
the ghosts of a town that had once been so busy
and alive.

Father and Lucas went into two more of the old buildings—a bank and a saloon—with Father taking pictures. Though this time he told the boys to stay out also. That crash seemed to have changed his mind about any young explorers who might well get into trouble.

"The interiors are in a better state than you would think," Christie heard him tell Lucas. "Maybe something can be done here after all that wouldn't cost a fortune. We could restore just the main attractions."

"I'm wondering about Gordon House—down there at the end of the street. It was considered quite a showplace in its day." Lucas pointed to a building that seemed larger and in better condition than those around it. The lower story was of stone and above that was a second floor of wood with a roofed balcony running along the whole front.

"Gordon built it and made it into a hotel. It was considered pretty fancy for that time and this place. It's probably been a shelter for every drifter passing through since then. But if it's storm tight, we'll need it—and soon."

"I'll take the car as close up as I can get it."

When the station wagon pulled up before the Gordon House, Christie was impressed. It seemed to have more life about it than the rest of the buildings. Lucas crossed the lower porch and pushed against double doors, the upper parts of which were filled in places with still unbroken panes of glass colored dark red, yellow, green, and blue.

The others followed him into a wide room that had a staircase up one side. In the middle was a big round seat with dusty cushions still on it. There was a desk with a pigeonholed wall cupboard behind, and tatters of lace curtains hung before the boarded-up windows. Lucas and Father both used flashlights and the gleam of those showed an archway into another room, where there were tables and chairs.

"Lobby, dining room— Even the old ledger was left." Lucas went to the desk and blew a cloud of dust off the big book lying there. "Wonder who registered last."

He opened the book, sending up more puffs of dust. "Let's see now—January nineteen twenty—just one entry—Philip Briggs, San Francisco."

"Now we'll make our entry legal." Lucas took a pen from his shirt pocket.

" 'April, nineteen eighty, Lucas Wildhorse, Libby Wildhorse, Toliver Wildhorse, Ten Mile Station, Arizona.' Your turn, Harvey."

He passed the pen to Father, who, smiling, wrote in turn, reading aloud as he went: " 'Harvey Kimball, Christie Kimball, Neal Kimball, Patrick and Patricia Kimball, Thai Shan Kimball, Baron Kimball, Ten Mile Station, Arizona.' "

"We may not be regular overnight guests,"

he added, "but I think we can make good use of a table and few chairs and—food—right now."

The rain broke so suddenly it was almost an explosion of water and wind. It pounded against the walls, drove in through the broken panes of the big door.

"We'll make a dash for the baskets. You children stay right here," Father ordered before he and Lucas ran for the station wagon. Luckily that had been parked close to the porch. Father and Lucas both had wet shirts before they were back with baskets and canteens.

"Here." Father tossed a roll of paper toweling to Christie. "You children wipe off one of the tables. Listen!" He paused and for a moment all they could hear was the wild drumming of the rain. "This sounds like a regular cloudburst. At least this place seems dry—if you keep away from the door."

The rain swept in through the broken panes almost as far as the round seat in the lobby. Now the whole of the inside of the hotel was very dark and gloomy. Even their flashlights were swallowed up into small glows.

Christie, as she dusted the nearest table, working beside Libby, with Neal and Toliver just across from her, found herself looking over her shoulder now and then into corners that seemed very dark indeed. But they were all here together—she was not alone—and they were safe out of the storm. She wadded up the dirty paper and left it on another table. Shan hissed fretfully and she picked him up to hold tight. There was nothing to be afraid of here—surely there was not.

11

The Sealed Valley

Lucas turned on a camp lantern like those they had used to explore the cave and it gave enough light for the long table through the gloom of the big room. After lunch Shan was the only one now who wanted to explore. He tugged at the leash Christie had put around a chair leg and demanded in sharp cries to be let loose.

"Must be mice here," Libby said.

"What would they eat?" Perks asked. "There's no food except what we have."

"Field mice," Libby explained. "They'd find their food outside but would live in here."

"We can't go out in this storm." Lucas had gone to the front door. "There's a regular flood running down the street. Might as well explore in here."

They repacked the picnic baskets and set out

180

to do just that. Behind the dining room was an even darker kitchen with a big stove, yellow with rust, and shelves on which were gathered a few pieces of thick china black with dust and dirt.

On the opposite side of the lobby, having passed through another archway, they found a long bar behind which hung the fragments of a mirror, most of which had been broken away. Some bottles still stood under that and there were more chairs and tables. At the other end of the room the lantern light struck a platform three steps above the regular floor, a curtain hanging in tatters on either side of that.

"Gave shows here, I suppose." Father took more camera shots with his light bulbs snapping, startling in the gloom.

From there they went up the stairs to the second floor, Lucas, in the lead, testing each step with care before he put his full weight upon it. There was a hall with doors open along it. Some of the rooms were empty. In one or two were beds with springs but no mattresses, and in some a washstand or a chest of drawers. All were dark because of shuttered windows along the front of the building.

Lucas paused before one door that was shut and had to put his shoulder to it before it came open. Rain instantly swept in and they looked out on the balcony above the street.

"Hey, all the rain's coming in!" Neal jumped

181

back and Christie expected Lucas to close the door. Instead he stood straining out until Father came out of another room.

"What's the matter?"

Now Lucas pulled the door shut. "Just taking a look," he said slowly. "Might be more damage after a burst like this one."

They went back downstairs while the rain came in fierce gusts. Father warned them to stay away from the windows—even those that were boarded up. Twice they heard loud crashes. Perks ran to Father and held on to him tightly, burying her face in his shirt. Baron cowered and whimpered. Shan used his claws to climb Christie as if she were a tree, hanging on to her shirt front, his ears flat against his head.

Father said he thought that some more of the old buildings must be breaking up under the pounding of the furious wind. Each storm in its time must add to the damage. Twice he went closer to the front door to look out at the station wagon. Once Neal crept along after him and came back to report that the water was running along halfway up the wheels of the car and the street looked like a river.

Runnels of the rain oozed in under the front doors as well as trickled from the broken panes. The dark red of the old carpet showed through in patches as the water washed the dust away.

"How long do these storms last?" Father finally asked Lucas.

The Navajo shrugged. "It's anyone guess. Though this is decidedly more forceful than usual."

"I don't like this!" Perks quavered. "I want to go home!"

"We can't drive through a rain like this," Neal told her.

"Come on, Perks." Christie put her arm about the younger girl. "Why this is a regular adventure. Aren't we lucky to have found so good a place to stay out of the storm? Oh— look at Shan!"

The cat had jumped from her shoulder only a moment ago, and was now crouched, only the tip of his outstretched tail quivering slightly as he crept forward very slowly, getting ready to spring on something only he could see. Then he pounced and sat for a moment, both fore-paws pinning down his prey.

"A mouse!" Christie hurried to rescue the captive and then stopped short with a cry of disgust as Shan's prisoner was shown to be, as he raised one paw, a very large black beetle.

"Nasty thing! You don't want that, Shan!" Christie used the edge of one of the newspapers they had spread for a tablecloth to flip the insect out of the way. Surely it was not the only one here and she began to agree with Perks that it would be better to get out of this dark, queer-smelling place and head home again.

Shan tugged at his leash, trying to follow the

scuttling beetle. Christie heard Baron barking at the door.

Lucas was talking to Father. "It's slacking off now. If this had lasted much longer it would have washed most of the town away."

The wind and the drum of the rain were lessening. It was not long before they were able to go out on the porch and look down the street to where the shrinking stream had cut new gullies in the earth, even carried away sections of the broken plank sidewalk.

"What's the matter with the road—up there?" Neal pointed to the rise down which they had driven into Darringer.

Christie took off her glasses, rubbed them dry on the tail of her shirt, and settled them once more on her nose, sure she had not seen properly before. The rise looked queer. Studying it, she was alarmed to see the road had gone! There was just a big hole there, as if half the ground had just disappeared! What had happened?

"Cave-in," said Lucas. He frowned and Father looked very sober.

"Is there another road out?"

"There could be. Rougher track that leads through the reservation. It's either try that or I walk out for horses and we come for the car later. There must have been a mine cutting under that ridge that brought it down when the ground loosened."

184

Did that mean they would have to stop here— maybe overnight? Christie shivered and drew nearer to Father. She did not want to be in Darringer in the full dark—the ghost town seemed more and more strange and threatening.

Father, looking up at the gray sky, a little lighter now, asked another question. "Is there liable to be another such downpour, do you think?"

Lucas was studying those same clouds. "I'd say no. Let me scout that other way out. The worst parts are those closest to town. Once we're through these hills the going's level—if rough. It will take us longer to get back, but I'd say it is the only way out after that landslip."

He rummaged in the car and brought out a square of waterproof plastic with a hole in the center for his head, and he tucked his Levi pants into his boots. Then he set out, jumping over the deep cuts made by the streams of water. Before he disappeared around the corner of the hotel he called back, "You'd better try the motor, to be sure it isn't flooded out."

"Will do!" Father looked at the children. "You," he told them in a no-argue voice, "stay right here."

As he splashed out to the station wagon, Perks's hand crept into Christie's.

"Chris—suppose—suppose we can't get home—"

"But we will!" Christie said in as sure a voice as she could use. "If we can't take the car, then Libby's father will be back with horses and we'll ride. That will be a real adventure! Of course we can get home all right!"

"I don't like adventures like this," Perks said doubtfully.

"Why don't we get the baskets and the canteens, and Shan, and have everything ready to load into the car?" Libby suggested. "Come on."

The boys did not follow, but Christie was glad Libby had thought of doing this. She was even ready to go, as long as Libby held the lighted camp lantern, into the big kitchen with the rubbish—packing that into the rusty stove while Libby lighted a match to burn it.

Afterward, they poured water over the stove fire and the charred remains of the rubbish. But the kitchen was so dark, they were very glad to go out on the porch again.

Father not only had the car running but had backed up and turned around to face in the direction Lucas had gone. Now he had a big map spread out on the steering wheel and was studying it. Seeing the girls, he beckoned to them.

"We might as well load up. We don't want to waste any time if the road out can be followed. There *is* a trail marked on this, but since it goes through the reservation, it will take us longer to get back to the station."

The last drizzle of rain had stopped. Water still dripped from the roofs of the houses and trickled in thinner streams down the road. They got in the car and waited. It was not too long before Lucas came again around the hotel and waved them on. Father drove slowly, stopping to pick him up.

"I think we have a clear road through the worst of the hill part," Lucas reported. "Also I do know the trail well enough to take that way. We had better get as far along as we can while it is still daylight."

The station wagon passed a barn. Half of the roof had fallen in and a mass of decayed hay hung over the edge of the break. Toliver pointed up and beyond that.

"There's an entrance to a mine—see?"

It was difficult to make out, but there was a square opening into a hillside and more half-ruined buildings. Christie held on to one side of the seat, Shan on her knees, while Libby and Perks clung to the other as the car dipped, bumped, and skidded a little, Father struggling with the wheel to hold it straight on a very narrow track.

Parky let out a whoop of excitement from the seat just behind. "Up and down—like the boop-doop in the park!"

"This isn't fun!" Christie turned on him. "Keep quiet, Parky!"

"Yes, shut up!" Neal snapped. "Don't yell in Dad's ears now!"

"You can't—" Parky began, when his brother swooped on him to place a hand firmly over his mouth, saying fiercely, "I can and will! You just keep quiet!"

He must have startled Parky, for the younger boy did not fight against his grip, only stared at his brother in astonishment. Christie closed her eyes and then opened them again. She did not know which was worse—to feel the car slipping around or to see the outside swing back and forth beyond its windows. There was a last bump and they crawled on without so much skidding. Now they were in a valley between two hills. Water still washed down the sides of those and was thrown back up by the wheels of the car.

As they were heading up a rise a little later, Christie heard Lucas say, "That sees us through the worst bit."

"I certainly hope so!" was Father's answer.

It was getting lighter. Finally the sun broke through the clouds. Christie sighed in relief. It made her feel better—and this road was not any bumpier than the one they had taken into Darringer.

"This is the old trail to Broken Tooth and Last Candle," Lucas said. "We turn off at a big rock that looks like a broken tooth. From then on we strike across country, taking our bearings on Tall Spur in the west.''

"I'll leave the guiding to you," Father told him. "This must be a long way around, though."

"It is. We can stop at the trader's at Two Rock if we have to. If the phone's out—it generally is after a storm such as this one—one of the boys there can take the upper trail and let them know at the station where we are and what happened. That's the best we can do."

"If it's the best, then that will have to be it," Father agreed.

Broken Tooth was indeed a queer-looking rock. Neal echoed Christie's thought when he said he thought it did not look much like a tooth.

"Not a human tooth," Lucas agreed. "but it does resemble the fang of a cougar with the tip broke off. Now, left here, Harvey."

Father obediently swung the station wagon out of the traces of the old trail onto the open land. However, they had gone only a little distance when Lucas called, "Pull up!"

Luckily Father had been going slowly. The front wheels were very close to a big cut across the ground. He and Lucas got out and walked along the ditch. It did not look deep from the car but Toliver, leaning against an open window frame, shook his head.

"Wash. Can't drive over that!"

"Why not?" Neal wanted to know.

"Sand's too soft. The wheels would just sink in."

The two men returned to the car. "You think we'd better turn back to the hills again?" Father was saying.

"I'd try that first." Lucas was facing the way they had come. "If we are to stay out tonight the hills are better than right here."

"Okay."

Again Father backed and turned cautiously. They crawled along a path that paralleled the wash for a while. Then the hills began to rise and the car stopped.

"This doesn't seem to be getting us anywhere."

"I agree. And it will be dark in another hour. We're boxed in. I can get overland to the Trading Post by morning, if I start soon. Then I can bring back help to bridge the wash. We'll have supper and I'll take off—"

"You're sure you can find your way in the dark?"

Lucas laughed at Father's question. "Harvey, I've ridden this country and walked it, too, since I was younger than Parky. You can't lose me in it. You may have to spend the night in the car—unless you want to go back to Darringer. But by morning I'll be back with help."

"Better stay here than go back to town," Father decided.

Again Christie sighed with relief. She did not

want to return to the ghost town. They had camped in the car before—it was far better than those falling-to-pieces houses back there.

"Good thing we brought plenty of supplies. Let's see what we have left in the baskets," Father suggested.

Toliver, Neal, and Parky had already spilled out of the car, Baron right at their heels. Libby and Christie passed the baskets over to Father, and then got out. Christie put Shan down on the ground and he walked stiff-legged, sniffing about.

"Get some wood, Toliver," his father said. "Neal can help you. Bring a lot. You should keep the fire going," he explained to Father. "Sometimes herders move in this direction and you might be able to get some help even before I get back. They'd come if they sighted a fire."

Toliver and Neal, Baron bounding ahead, scrambled toward the rising ground where there was a growth of trees and brush. Lucas took out a pair of field glasses. With these slung around his neck he climbed to the roof luggage carrier and used them to look westward.

Father was examining the contents of the baskets, dividing the food left into two lots. "Supper"—he pointed out to one—"and this we'll put back for breakfast."

He had just begun to do that when Neal came running down the slips. He was not carrying any wood—instead he waved his arms excitedly over his head. Father dropped a packet of sandwiches and took a quick step in his direction.

"What is the—"

"Come and see! Come and see!" Neal's last bound brought him close enough to be able to pull at Father's arm. He was gasping, so he had little breath left with which to explain.

Lucas jumped from the top of the car and hurried along behind Father and Neal. Christie saw Libby was also following. She stopped only long enough to fasten Shan's leash to the door handle (which made him yowl loudly) and went after the rest, catching Perks's hand as she steadied the younger girl.

They all had to slow down when they came around the side of the hill, for there was a tumble of stones and earth. It looked rather like the stopper that had been used to close the treasure cave. Father caught at Neal with one hand and Parky with the other.

"Take it easy! You could have a nasty fall here."

"Another landslip. The storm must have brought this down, too." Lucas kicked at a stone. "What's so exciting?" he asked Neal.

It was Toliver, standing on a big rock farther on, who cried out now, urging them to join him.

However, Lucas and Father went slowly, holding back both Parky and Neal, who were fairly dancing with impatience. Baron flashed by the rock on which Toliver was perched and began barking very loudly indeed.

"Look there!"

The landslip had opened a narrow door into a valley. But facing them there was what was so astounding, though at first Christie was puzzled at what she saw. What was so important about an old broken wagon? Then she saw it was not really a wagon after all.

"It's a stagecoach!" Neal shouted, his voice echoing down the valley. "Stagecoach! Stagecoach!"

"And it says Bright Line on the door!" Toliver leaped from his rock perch and went to thump on the door of the coach.

Lucas joined him, shining his flashlight into the interior. A moment later he released his hold on the window sill and slid down. Then he walked to the front of the mass of wood, leather, and rusted metal.

Father climbed over to join him. Lucas said something to Father and handed him the torch. Then Father crawled up to look through the same window.

"It's the ghost coach they tell the story about, I bet!" Neal declared. "The Indians must have chased it here and—"

"Not Indians, I think," Father said as he came back to them. "Though in a way it is a

ghost coach. No, its being here is not, I believe, the result of an Indian attack."

"But—but weren't they running, and got caught?" To Christie that seemed the only explanation.

"No. This coach must have been purposely hidden, all right. However, that was done to cover up another crime. I'm afraid that the driver who promised those passengers a run through the Indian attack lines was more a danger to those who bribed him than any Apaches. He must have brought the coach near here—if the passengers did not know the country they would not suspect him of a detour when he explained it was to escape capture. Then he robbed his passengers and—perhaps he had a confederate—he or they could take the horses and escape."

"But the passengers—" Christie asked.

"They are still in the coach," Father answered. "Whoever killed them must have then walled the coach up here. And during all this time it was hidden until the flood brought the landslip today. I'm afraid this particular crime will never be solved—it occurred too far in the past."

Christie backed away from the coach. This surely *must* be the ghost coach that was supposed to run along the old road at night. She turned, pulling Perks with her, and hurried back toward the car. Father caught up with her and dropped a comforting, warm hand on her shoulder.

"There's nothing here now to disturb anyone, Chris. It all happened a very long time ago."

"I know," she answered. "But they said that the ghost coach goes along the road at night. Maybe it will come out of here tonight—"

"Christie!" Her father's hold on her tightened, holding her fast. "There are all kinds of queer old stories that people like to tell just to scare themselves and others. This coach won't be going anywhere—tonight or any other night. We won't go in there again. Now—let's go back to camp, get a fire started, and have supper. We'll sleep in the car, just as we have other nights—all together and safe. There is nothing to be afraid of—nothing!"

Christie relaxed. With Father right here she knew she was being silly. Of course he was right—there was nothing to be afraid of now.

"Maybe—maybe because we found Lady Maude and the other things, that's why we found the coach, too." She said the first thing that slipped into her mind. "Maybe they all go together."

Father's arm hugged her. "Could be you're right. Stranger things have happened—"

"I'm hungry, good and hungry." Parky

joined them. "Let's go and get something to eat. That old coach isn't going anywhere now."

Father laughed. "Right you are, Parky."

A moment later Christie was able to laugh, too. She was hungry, too, now that she did not feel so queer and cold inside.

12
Lady Maude Goes Home

Christie sat beside Mother, nervously folding and unfolding her hands. They felt sticky even though the big studio was so cool. Mr. Simmons had told them earlier what questions he was going to ask, and they had practiced their answers several times. But she still wished the program was all over. She was so afraid she would say something wrong, or forget. She and Libby were to hold up Lady Maude and then open the little trunks and boxes before the TV cameras. Then the cameras would switch over to Toliver and Neal, who would talk about the strongbox and the shotgun. Shan should really have been here, too, since he had found the cave, but they were sure he would have been too frightened.

After they did that, their part in the program

would be over. Then the postmaster was going to talk about the mail bag and Mr. Simmons about Ten Mile Station. Last of all, Sheriff Wylie would describe the coach they had found near Darringer three days before. Tonight they were to stay at a motel here in town so they could see themselves on TV—which would be exciting—once this was safely over.

Father was to have been here too, but he had to drive to the airport to pick up Mr. Colby. Christie looked at Libby, who was also sober-faced. Maybe inside she was just as uncertain as Christie. They must forget about the camera, Mr. Simmons had told them—just make believe they were talking only to him as they had been when they had practiced.

"Ready—" Mr. Simmons beckoned from the table, where the bright lights were centered.

Christie got up. At first she felt her legs were shaking far too much for her to walk at all. Libby's hand caught hers in a very tight hold. They reached the chairs they had sat in during the rehearsal. Christie put out a finger to touch Lady Maude where the doll stood, with a stand to hold her securely upright. What did she think about all this? Christie wondered.

She swallowed the lump that seemed to fill her throat as she heard Mr. Simmons begin the familiar story of how they found the cave. Then, altogether too quickly, he began his questions. Libby's was first and she answered it—her name and where she lived. Then Christie said the same. She kept watching Lady Maude, and somehow, with her eyes on the doll, she was not so frightened. She opened the jewel case and her share of the bags, while Libby spread out the other parts of Lady Maude's wardrobe.

The lights winked out and Mr. Simmons waited for them to pack away the lady and her things. Then Neal and Toliver took the girls' places to talk about their part of the finds. Christie was glad to be back again beside Mother.

When the program was over, they met Father in front of the broadcasting station. He had Mr. Colby with him, and also a tall man who thanked Father for the lift as he climbed out of the car.

"This is my wife and family, and their friends, Libby and Toliver Wildhorse," Father said. "Patricia, children, this is Congressman Cranford. He is interested in Jemez Park. I've been telling him about the station and the finds."

Mr. Cranford had gray hair and Christie thought him stern-looking until he smiled. "I am most pleased to have the chance to meet you, Mrs. Kimball. Now, let me see." He turned to the children. "Here are the heroines and heroes of the treasure hunt—but aren't there more of you?"

"Perks and Parky are with Mrs. Wildhorse," Neal told him. "They went to see the Indian exhibit in the bank lobby."

"Perks and Parky, and you must be Neal Kimball. Then—ladies—" He held out his hand first to Libby and then to Christie. "Miss Libby and Miss Christie—and this is Toliver—am I right?"

"And," he continued, glancing at the precious box that Libby and Christie carried between them, "can this be part of the treasure in question?"

"It's Lady Maude and her things," Christie answered shyly.

"Lady Maude! I understand she is to appear on a special TV program tonight. Do you suppose I may have a private interview with the lady later on?"

"We have to take her back to Sheriff Wylie's office," Christie explained. "He's keeping her until he finds out who really owns her."

"I see. Well, perhaps the sheriff will let us get together. Such a famous and far-traveled lady should not have to spend most of her time shut up in a box. It has been a great pleasure, and I trust that this will not be the last time we meet." He smiled at them again and raised his hat.

When they got into the car and Mr. Cranford had gone into the broadcasting studio, Christie heard Mr. Colby say to Father, "Wonder what brought him out here at this time. Oh, I know he's on the park committee, but usually an eastern congressman is not going to travel to see a national park clear out here. As far as I know no one was expecting to see him. He's traveling alone, not on official business."

"I only know what you heard him say." Father did not appear too interested. "How did the program go, Pat?"

"They were all a little nervous, understandably, but once it started they did very well, as you shall for yourself this evening. Here's the sheriff's office—we'll take Lady Maude in and be right back. Christie and Libby can go—you boys stay in the car."

Only the young man who used the typewriter was there. He took Lady Maude's box and gave them a receipt. Then they went on to the motel. Christie was unhappy. If only Lady Maude could have come with them!

"I wish she could have a real home," she told Libby, who seemed to understand. "It must be very dull for her to be shut in that box day after day."

"Dull for a doll?" Neal had overheard her, much to Christie's instant annoyance. "A doll isn't alive, doesn't know what is going on. You're crazy."

"Lady Maude isn't just a doll." Christie tried to put her feelings into words. "She's—she's like a real person." Neal only laughed at her again and she was sorry she had said that. He would never understand the way she was sure Libby did.

Mother insisted on an afternoon rest time for the twins so they could sit up and watch the program in the evening. Neal and Toliver went off on their own to see the Indian exhibit at the bank. Christie and Libby had books to read and the motel room was cool and comfortable, but Christie felt restless.

If they could only be sure things would come out all right! She had what some people considered a bad habit of always looking at the last few pages of a new book before she read it, just to be sure that it had a happy ending. She never enjoyed the other sort. Now there was no way of turning to the final page in their own story to make sure it finished well. They would just have to wait for the end. She was afraid that was *not* going to go right. It could so well be a hurting one, with them moving away from the station—never able to see Libby and Toliver again—and perhaps even watching Lady Maude being given to Marlene!

Libby moved across the sofa and put her hand lightly on Christie's arm, shaking her out of her gloomy thoughts for a moment or two. "Did you see Marlene? She was across the street when we came out of the studio. When she watches the program tonight, she's going to be really mad."

"Why?"

"Because we're in it and she isn't. She probably thinks if she could have taken Lady Maude she would have been in our place there today."

Christie counted days on her fingers. It had been a whole week since she had mailed the letter to Maine. How much longer would she have to wait before she knew if anyone would answer it?

"Christie, where will your family go if you have to move away from the station?" Libby's question cut through her thoughts.

"I don't know."

"If Mr. Colby decides to build up the ghost town, perhaps you could go there."

Darringer? Christie shook her head. She did not want to live there even if the old houses could be rebuilt. Anyway, there was no longer any way in since the landslide. There was only the back trail they had come out on after Libby's father had brought men from the Trading Post to help the station wagon over the wash. That was too bad for any tourists to want to travel.

"I hope you stay somewhere around here," Libby went on. "We could go to school together in the fall. I'm in the sixth grade now."

"So'm I. Or I was going to be. We left school early to drive out. But Mother has our books and once we settle in we're to do some work each day this summer so we can start where we're supposed to. Neal would go to junior high. And the twins start in second."

How far "back home" seemed now. Would they return? Christie found herself wishing they would not. She did not like waiting to decide things—she never had. She wanted to read the last page and right *now!*

They had supper in a restaurant and went back to the motel to wait for the TV program. In the lobby they met Mr. Cranford again. He was talking to Lucas Wildhorse and looked around at them with one of his face-warming smiles when they came in.

"This is a big night for you, isn't it?" he asked the children. "Mr. Wildhorse has taken pity on a stranger and has very kindly asked me to join you to watch the program. I hope you don't mind?"

Why did he want to? Christie wondered. But she did not have time to think about that very long, for he had come directly to her to say, "I have spoken to Sheriff Wylie and he says that if you are willing we can go to his office tomorrow and you can unpack Lady Maude for me. I have a daughter at home—she's some years older than you and Libby, but not too old to enjoy hearing about Lady Maude, who, I am sure, is not an ordinary doll at all."

For some reason Christie did not feel at all shy with Mr. Cranford. "No," she answered promptly. "Lady Maude is extra special. I don't think there is another doll like her in the whole world now!"

"You are probably very right, Christie," he agreed.

"Harvey," Lucas said to her father, "you might be interested in a couple of things Congressman Cranford has to say about Jemez."

"I trust you will." Mr. Cranford turned back to the older people, while Christie and Libby sat down on a settee in the lobby.

Mr. Charvez, the owner of the motel, had pulled the big TV set out a little, and the boys were helping him bring in extra chairs. Some of the guests had gathered to wait for the program. Why, Christie realized, they were going to have a regular audience when the time came to watch. Then Mr. Charvez turned out all the lights except the one behind the desk so they could see better.

Christie grasped Mother's hand tightly. Had they really done their speeches all right? Or would people laugh?

There was the announcer talking about Mr. Simmons, and then Mr. Simmons himself talking to the postmaster, showing off the old letters and the mailbag. Christie squirmed. She was eager, yet a little frightened, to see Libby and herself on the screen.

Now Mr. Simmons again.

"The two young ladies who had a part in the

discovery of this unique find—Miss Christie Kimball and Miss Libby Wildhorse—".

There they were. It was very queer to see yourself sitting talking when you knew you were here watching. But she had been all right. None of the shakiness she had felt showed. She was answering Mr. Simmons's questions in a voice you could hear clearly, showing off the parts of Lady Maude's wardrobe as he asked her to. And Libby was as good.

Then their part was over and the boys followed. It went smoothly for them also.

"Now"—Mr. Simmons was nearing the end— "I have another part of this story, an even more recent discovery, which will be told by Sheriff James Wylie. Sheriff Wylie—"

He told about finding the stagecoach and how it might even be the ghost coach of the old stories. He added what they suspected might be the true story—that the passengers had been driven off and killed for what they were carrying on their persons—but that might never be proven now.

The program came to an end and Mr. Charvez put the lights on. Then the other people staying in the motel gathered around the Kimballs and the Wildhorses to ask questions. Then Mother shooed the children off to their own rooms. She and Libby and Perks shared one room, the boys another.

"Chris," Libby asked through the dark, "do

you think Mr. Cranford wants Lady Maude? Maybe the government will take her.''

Christie had not thought of that before. ''I don't know,'' she answered unhappily.

Tomorrow seemed a long way off, but Christie was more sleepy than she had thought and it was suddenly morning.

Mother and Father did not go the sheriff's office with Christie and Libby—they had business with Mr. Colby. But Mr. Cranford came to pick them up in a rented car. Sheriff Wylie took them into a small side room where Lady Maude's box waited on a table.

'' 'Miss Maude Woodbridge, Woburnscott, Maine,' '' Mr. Cranford read off the lettering. ''She had a long way to travel, didn't she? And she never got home after all.''

''She came from Hong Kong,'' Christie said, ''and that's a long way, too. Clear from the other side of the ocean. And before that from France—''

''How do you know all that?''

Christie hesitated. The letter was no secret any longer. Still, it should have been turned over with those in the bag. However, she might as well tell.

''There was a letter inside the box. It was from Captain Asa Woodbridge to his little girl. He said that Lady Maude had been sent to Hong Kong from France for another little girl. Only when Lady Maude got there that girl had

209

gone. So he bought Lady Maude to bring her here for his daughter's birthday. Then when he got to San Francisco there was another ship he had to sail on. so he sent Lady Maude with the mate from his ship who was going home.''

"Where is this letter?"

Christie looked at Lady Maude. "I sent it to Maine. You see, Daddy said they would try to find the families of the people to whom those other letters were written. I wanted Lady Maude to go to her real home. If we couldn't keep her for our plan—"

"What plan?"

Again Christie hesitated, glancing from the doll to Mr. Cranford. "It was what we thought we could do to help make people want to stop at the station. We thought of making a kind of museum with things people would want to see. Then we could put up signs on the highway advertising it. We were hunting for arrowheads to use when we found Lady Maude and all the rest. For a while we hoped we could keep the things and have them to show. Then Mr. Toner—he—well—" The rest spilled out in a rush of words—the claim on the station, Marlene's demand to be given Lady Maude.

"So," Christie ended, "I wrote a letter about how we found Lady Maude and I put it with the old letter and sent it. But I haven't heard anything and maybe there is no one to get it now."

"It has come back." Mr. Cranford took from his own coat pocket the fat letter Christie had taken so long to write. It bulged even more for the top had been cut open and she could see the brownish paper of the old letter among her sheets.

"But how—"

"You were right, or your father was, about the families concerned with the old letters being notified. Luckily I was in Woburnscott when this arrived, so the postman brought it straight to me."

"But you're not named Woodbridge," Libby protested.

"No, but my grandmother was Maude Woodbridge, before she married Rufus Cranford. Captain Asa Woodbridge was my great-grandfather. My daughter is Maude Woodbridge Cranford and many people think she looks very much like that other Maude for whom this birthday gift was intended. Even more exciting than the finding of Lady Maude herself—though you may not believe this—is the letter.

"You see, for all these years my grandmother never knew what had happened to her father. He was supposed to have started east, but, though time and money was spent searching for him, he was never found. Now we know it was his mate who was coming overland, using the stage ticket the captain had bought in his own name. The ship in which he had come from Hong Kong was, as he said in this letter, sold to a firm in South America. He took the place of another captain who had died of fever. The records of the company in San Francisco did not say that. There was a fire there and the company went bankrupt as a result, their records lost in the fire. While the ship the captain had taken was never heard of again after it sailed. We still have a mystery, but not an unpleasant one now."

"Unpleasant?" Christie wondered.

Mr. Cranford nodded. "Yes, you see it was thought that Captain Asa was carrying quite a large sum of money for the company. In fact it was the loss of that money that added to the bankruptcy of the company. By the evidence of this letter he must have given the money to his mate and it was stolen in the stagecoach holdup. The mate must have made the mistake of letting someone know what he carried when he bribed the driver to take out the missing stage. Now, after all these years, we have proof that it was not Captain Asa who disappeared with the money."

"Then Lady Maude is yours?" Christie fingered the little jewel case reluctantly.

"Let us say that Lady Maude is a Woodbridge, yes. But her final home is not yet decided. However, do you suppose you can set her up, spread out all her treasures, so I can take some pictures? I promised Maude to send her a set as soon as I could."

Christie and Libby went to work, and Mr. Cranford took a number of pictures with his Polaroid camera. Libby and Christie viewed these critically and selected the best.

"Now, for the present we can return her to Sheriff Wylie's care and go mail these off to Maude. After that I have a conference with your father, Mr. Colby and Mr. Wildhorse, and you are all to be my guests at lunch. I have a very great deal to thank you for, and especially you, Christie, for having the enterprise to send the letter."

It was not until they had finished lunch that they heard the rest of the story. Mr. Cranford looked around the table. There were so many in their party that the restaurant had given them a side room to themselves, and, when the door was closed, it was quiet and private.

Mr. Cranford pushed his coffee cup to one side as they waited for him to speak.

"I am what you term a history buff," he began, "and for the younger members here who may not know what that means, I will just say that I like history very much. So it was a pleasure for me to find a place, while serving in Congress, on a committee that deals with the preservation and conservation of our historical sites.

"Though I come from New England, the

western part of the country has long interested
me. Perhaps because at the end of the Civil
War two of my great-uncles came west and
helped in the growth of this very state of Arizona. For all I know, they may have traveled
on the Bright coaches and stayed overnight at
Ten Mile Station. The opening of the new highway to the Jemez National Park will make this
part of the country available to those who want
to see something of the Old West.

"The plan you, Kimball and Colby, have in
mind is the type of thing that needs fostering—
the rebuilding and maintenance of part of our
historical heritage. Since I have been informed
of the situation—the legal tangle—now facing
you, I think matters can be worked out. Water
rights can be shared if care is taken.

"The TV program yesterday, which I have
been since informed was picked up to become
a national broadcast, will be beneficial—not
only for your project, but for attracting attention to the park area in general. I have already
called Senator Meegan and your local congressman.

"Now as to the things found in the cave.
While the mail must go through regular chan-
nels, the mailbag itself and the strong box—
minus its contents—plus the luggage is a different matter. These articles could be put on
display at Ten Mile Station. The stage found
in the valley can perhaps be restored and

moved also to Ten Mile to exhibit. These are all just suggestions."

He paused for a sip of coffee. "About the actual ownership of Ten Mile—the lawyers will have to look into the facts concerning that. It may be that the title can never be really cleared. The Navajo council also has a claim to put forward. However, it can be that a very long-term lease might be had—which would satisfy most of you. And I have been informed that suggestion has already been most favorably considered by your local court and the Navajo council.

"We come now"—he smiled at Libby and Christie—"to the matter of the lady who has waited a long time to enter the world again. In fact, she is not unlike the fairy tale Sleeping Beauty, is she not, girls? Lady Maude's future *is* mine to settle since my family can claim her. It is my decision that she is to remain here, under the joint guardianship of Christie Kimball and Libby Wildhorse. If a museum does become part of Ten Mile, she is to be put on display there. If, for some reason, that is impossible, her guardians shall determine where she will go, but this is to be her home. Christie and Libby shall make a report once a year to my daughter concerning Lady Maude and her welfare.

"Though we cannot make any final decisions yet, I believe that matters can be arranged in

fairness for all. Now I wish to propose a toast—
in what seems an excellent brand of cola—"
He stood up and brought from a side table a
tray of glasses, passing one to each of them.
"A toast," he repeated, "to Ten Mile Station,
and its future success!"

Christie drank. Lady Maude had not been
unlucky after all! Instead she had been their
good luck! If it had not been for her, all the rest
might not have happened. The others were all
talking. But Christie sat quietly until Libby
reached out to her.

"It was your letter really—"

"Maybe," Christie answered contentedly.
"Only Lady Maude really did it, didn't she?
Oh, Libby, it will be fun giving her a place
of her own at Ten Mile! People will love seeing her. We can put different dresses on her
and—"

"And everything!" Libby finished for her.
"Christie, it's going to be just wonderful at Ten
Mile!"

"Young ladies!"

They both looked up, startled. Mr. Cranford
stood there.

"I have made the necessary arrangements
with Sheriff Wylie. He's prepared to surrender
Lady Maude to you, and you can take her home
this afternoon. But remember—I expect to be
hearing from you about just how she conducts
herself and how things go for her."

"Yes, oh, yes, Mr. Cranford! We'll remember!" Christie promised.

She looked around for Mother or Father—maybe they could go right now to collect Lady Maude. She would really feel much safer to be back at Ten Mile with Lady Maude. That was *home* for all of them, now and forever, ever more! Christie hugged that thought to her very tightly indeed.

ABOUT THE AUTHOR

ANDRE NORTON is a highly acclaimed author of science fiction and fantasy. She has had over seventy books published in the United States and abroad, and her novels have appeared in several languages. Miss Norton has received numerous writing and science fiction awards, including the Gandalf Award for "Life's Work in Fantasy". She was the first woman writer to become a member of the Swordsmen and Sorcerers Guild. Her other Archway titles include the *Star Ka'at* series (written with Dorothy Madlee), *Steel Magic, Fur Magic, Octagon Magic* and *Seven Spells to Sunday* (written with Phyllis Miller).